Under Construction

Under Construction

Natalie Yaipen

Natalie Yaipen
2020

Library of Congress Cataloging-in-Publication Data:
A catalog record for this book is available from the Library of Congress.

ISBN 978-0-578-64608-4

Book Cover Design by emulsify

Contents

Acknowledgements

I am deeply thankful to Penélope, Kimberly, and Dr. Goins for supporting me and encouraging me to go on this journey. When I first thought of the book and my reasons behind it, you encouraged me to put my voice out into the world.

Thank you to my friends, my sisters, my Momentum family, and my Leadership Team and coaches for your patient guidance and encouragement. You led me to push beyond doubt, to embrace my creativity, and to trust my work.

Many deepest gratitude for my family. Thank you for believing in me, investing in me, and loving me. You have been by my side, seen my busy days and late nights, and never doubted my ability to do this. You reminded me on the difficult days why I started it in the first place.

Thank you, Patrick, for challenging my writing and supporting my creative process. Thank you for reading the countless drafts and offering suggestions and edits.

This book was able to be completed with everyone's support and guidance. Thank you.

Prologue

I was in my last year of college when I realized I wanted to forward a message. Something I've heard said many times: "It is NOT your fault..." But I want to add and emphasize a part: "...even if it has happened to you more than once."

I am a survivor of sexual violence.

Five years ago, I was walking home at night. Reflecting on the fact that, yet again, I was frustrated, because I had a canceled therapy session, that I did not ask to be canceled. That I had to spend energy and effort just to even find out it was canceled. That it was still difficult for me to even get up and go to therapy in the first place.

No one was forcing me to go, but on the walk to the clinic, I felt watched, ashamed, and guilty. I had this amazing Women's Studies professor who would just listen to me. I could hear her voice telling me not to hold shame. It wasn't mine to carry. That night, I remembered the mentors I've had who, in different ways, have told me and other young survivors a similar thing.

This book comes from having experienced sexual violence, knowing loved ones from all ages share their stories with me and seeing that, while the act of violence may have passed, we all faced a different battle afterward.

I decided to share that battle, which is where the story of Amira Luisa comes in -- a young girl who goes through life trying to understand what is happening, what she wants, and what she deserves in this life. She is more than what's happened to her.

An Introduction

Under Construction is a recollection of memories and how they lead Amira Luisa, an abuse survivor, to her own self-acceptance.

Every so often, some thing, some place, or some person may lead her to feel overwhelmed, panicked, sad, or defensive. It may also cause fatigue or loss of appetite or the feeling of wanting to disconnect. Sometimes, it lasts for a few seconds but at times, those feelings can linger. She may not always know when or why it happens, but she is present to her inner voice. These stories were not written with the intention of causing a negative emotional response. That said, they will be touching on adverse experiences that individuals may remember from their own personal adverse experiences. Throughout the book, you will find phrases meant as a "pause" to check in with yourself. They were created with Love.

Love Note #0

Recollections may be triggering for survivors.

Please take care of yourself first.

*Section titles will have * for warning.*

Love Note #1

You will find Love Notes throughout the book. These Love Notes are meant to offer space for reflection. A space where we get the opportunity to sit with what was just read or about to be read. To not hold judgment for ourselves or Amira but to hold love, compassion, and curiosity.
~ *Natalie*

I: An Innocent Life

Amira Luisa

Dear Workbook,   April 2, 2004

It's easier to write here because *mami* won't look at the back of my book. Oh! But all I want is for the summer to arrive already. I'm bored... I can't wait for sixth grade to be over! Last summer was so much fun! We spent so much time in the arcade. And roller coaster rides!

And guess what? Cristal and I only had one major fight.

Ugh...that fight... she just stomped off and got lost! I had to go looking for her with our friend.

I am so ready for days in the sun, *papi* on the grill, *mami* sitting by the table, and Cristal, Angel, Catalina and I playing outside. Correction... My siblings: Catalina, Angel, and Cristal will be outside playing basketball.

I, Amira Luisa, do not play sports.

Actually, poor Catalina. The basketball hoop is already attached to the garage. Cristal and Angel are gonna be doing layups, while Catalina is begging them to get the volleyball net.

Sigh... Workbook, I'm tired of being in school. I'm ready for summer vacation! But I'll at least take spring break first.

School Pin

Dear Workbook,   April 7, 2004

It's been a day and I just need a place to say that I am so tired of wearing this uniform.

Another day of wearing the ugly plaid skirt with the button-up, long

5

sleeve T. Who thought they would look good together??? All I want is my N.U.T. cards -- NO UNIFORM TODAY. Imagine if I had one for every day of the school year? Maybe Mr. Tree wouldn't have been on my case:

Mr. Tree goes, "Amira, where's your school pin?"
Rolling my eyes, I say, "I didn't want to wear it."
Mr. Tree voice "You already don't have the proper shoes, so please put the pin on if you have it."

If I had wanted a call home, I would have just smiled and ignored Mr. Tree. But considering that art club was happening that afternoon, I couldn't risk it. Being stuck at home with Angel and Catalina instead of being surrounded by all my paintbrushes, colors, palettes, and paper. I'm not stupid; I had to make a choice.

My Happy Place -- the brown-colored cafeteria only filled with people like me who loved art. Some music playing from the school speakers. Me laughing with friends and creating.

Besides, Cristal had basketball practice, so she was staying too. Then again… it's easier for our parents if both of us are sticking together. See that's what happens when a couple has children three years apart, but their last two kids are twins.

Yea, I wasn't risking a call home. Angel and Catalina could have the study space to themselves for today.

Be Like…

Dear Workbook,   May 7, 2004

"Be like Catalina. She's smart, athletic, friendly with all, loved by all," my mom would say.

Thanks. That's exactlyyyy what I want – to be another Catalina. Another skinny arm, flat stomach, light brown and blonde highlights

Eva Mendes lookalike. (I mean, I liked her in the *2 Fast 2 Furious* movie, but no thank you.)

I looked at mom's eyes, my shoulders slouched a bit and I just said, "no thanks," while I looked down.

I rather be Amira Luisa. I'm not 10 anymore, I'm 12 years old now, I can stand on my own. Just Amira. Not 'Catalina's little sister.' Not 'aw Angel's kid sister.'

Does she understand I hear this every day in school?
Why should I be like them? Can't I just be me?

"Amira!! Put the book down and come eat!" mom yelled.
"Hold on! Let me finish the chapter"
"*Ahora!*," she screamed.
"*Ahyyy, Voyyy!*"

Sheesh! And the book was just getting good! But of course, *mami* wants me to stop. When I want to read more, I'm being disobedient, and I get yelled at. But I'm supposed to be smart, right? So why can't I just read?

Love Note #2

Every person should have the right to be their own person. Without being compared to anyone else. Be that a sibling, cousin, relative, friend.

You have every right to be yourself.

Burning Candles

Dear Workbook,   May 9, 2004

Another night of Catalina calling us to come eat. Cristal has to get the napkins. Angel is supposed to get the forks, but of course, he leaves it for either me or Cristal to do. I bring the cups. *Mami* puts out the food she cooked for us. Never late. And everyone takes a seat. *Papi,* at the head of the table.

And the candles.

...who gets to light them??

The silver candle set up, with cloth underneath it. Very Catholic. Four candles all dedicated to Jesus and what He is supposed to bring to this world - hope, love, joy, and peace. If you looked at it, you would think it's only supposed to be out for Advent.

But for us, Workbook, it's always out. Every family dinner. Because we wish for those things every day. No one has to put them out.

But who gets to light them?
Only mom and dad.
We can't touch the fire.

I mean...what's the worst that could happen? God forbid we get burned.

Tonight, Catalina was talking to *papi* about her classes. She's in college now so it's important. I mean I didn't understand everything they were talking about, but I know she studies hard. She's always in that little room in the basement. It's like her private little cave. Since she's the first in the family to go to college, that means she gets her own space to focus. I was just looking down at my plate and eating a fork-full of chicken and rice. There's nothing that I could've said to add to this conversation yet.

Then Angel and his spikey hair were going on and on about his football team. *Mami* looked so concerned...She's probably praying he doesn't get a concussion out there. Haha... she doesn't have to worry about me there. Grab another fork full of food. Drink some juice.

Oh yeah, Cristal was trying to get *mami*'s attention too with her team.
I think she plays tennis now? Or maybe she's still in basketball… I'm
not sure. I can't keep up with what sport she's playing.

Then there's me, Workbook. What am I doing if not just watching
everybody else?

First Fridays

Dear Workbook,   May 13, 2004

Here we go again.
Like the school motto goes: we must "dare the impossible
and live the vision!"

… I'm beginning to think it's more so *their* vision.

And listen Workbook. I'm not rude! But it gets a little repetitive…
Every first Friday of the month, we always begin at church.
We move slowly, aisle by aisle. We walk to the back of the
classroom. As we head into the thin walk-in, class closet, each of us
grabs our coats off the hooks. We exit, like robots, through the door at
the other end of the closet and make two lines at the front of the class.
Girls on one line, boys on the other.

Enter stage right,
Exit stage left.

Then we walk across the Courtyard….which is really just the teacher
parking lot. We go through the yellow doors, then up the stairs, then
the brown leather doors. Another hour lecture? … no… Gospel.

Lessons and "guidance" offered to us Catholic school kids, so we can
behave. I got other words for it that aren't Gospel. I call it the "you
better do as you are told" rules the monsignor loves to give.

There is never a month where we don't set the "intentions and expectations" for the month.

Workbook, there are days that I get why we are always told what to do but... I sometimes wish I knew for myself what I want to do. I know what I like to do but it's just like at home. Mom and dad are always telling us to eat certain fruits because they are good for losing weight or telling us to be like someone else. It's like everyone always wants us to be something they imagine or want us to be like.

Graphite

Dear Workbook,   May 18, 2004

Angel's friend goes "Amira, why don't you play softball? That way your family has volleyball, basketball, and softball covered."

Um...

I just look around at my siblings.

"Mine!"

Catalina called the ball after it was served, going for a perfect set.

Swishhhh

Angel's basketball went through the hoop. The crowd ROARSSS.

Laughing loudly, I look at Angel's friend and point at my glasses.
"Do you WANNNTTT me to lose an eye?"
"I'll stick to my HB, 2B, 4B, 6B pencils and sketchbook..."

It was easier to stay in the background. No one worried about the quiet (mainly good) girl. No one needs to hear me, but that doesn't mean I can't be heard.

Love Note #3

Being who you are in a space where everyone else seems to be the same can feel lonely. Be you regardless. You offer uniqueness wherever you are. You give off a light they may not understand yet.

Like a Pig

Dear Workbook,   May 20, 2004

Today, Cristal and I were eating chips.

Now I don't know about Cristal, but I was chowing them down like there was no tomorrow. At least until I got told, "you eat like a pig."

Let me tell you how good it does NOT feel to be judged!

Cristal and I were shocked! Stunned! I could feel the tears at the edges of my eyes.

This time it was someone else telling me it.
I let the tears come down like a rainstorm; my cries being the lightning. But Workboook, why did I cry if I say it to myself every day? It was different than those times. It doesn't feel the same coming from someone else.

"Why doesn't [X] like me?"
-   Because your stomach goes over your skirt
-   Because you haven't gotten one that fits a little looser
-   Because your arms are a little too thick
-   Because they're too manly looking
-   Because you look horrible in the white, button-up uniform

Why would they like you when they can have little Miss Popular over there? The one with skinny arms, perfect white straight teeth, and a

11

smile that is so contagious everyone wants to be around.

Workbook,
I'm the nerdy friend.
The quiet friend.

Let me stay with my books. After all, this tuition won't pay for itself.
I need that scholarship.

Today was just another day. Another day, another aunt making
comments about our weight. I didn't bother to talk to Cristal about
how she felt. She's like that girl Yoli from the movie we watched last
week, *Gotta Kick It Up*. The cargo pants, the t-shirt, the grimace. All
of it. And just like her, when someone makes an ugly comment
because she was eating a peanut butter cup, she says nothing and
doesn't care.

I'm not like her. I don't want to tell Cristal that I believe the things our
aunts say.

Plus, I say meaner things to myself every other day (if not every day).

Today though? Today I enjoyed my chips. My wonderful honey
barbecue Lays chips.

To spite my aunt, I licked the BBQ powder off my fingers when I was
done. It was priceless, seeing her face of disgust. "A lady does not act
that way."

Too bad. There's more where that came from.

So Sweet

Dear Workbook,   May 21, 2004

"Amira, your brother is over there," Bridges says with her googly
eyes.

I look at Angel and then look at her. Laughing, I gave her the 'get over yourself' look.

"Barf."
When will I be able to be in school without my friends falling in love with my brother?
"Gag. Gross."
Haha but this is what happens when they think he's cute. Him with his spikey hair, extra extra Large Ts, and shortly grown mustache that makes him look like George Lopez. Bridges wasn't the only one but was one of the first.

"Oh, c'monnn let me look at Angel. Don't pretend like you don't look at Byron," says Bridges.

"Byron isn't your BROTHERR though"

Bridges laughs as she wraps her arms around me to try and tease me.

"Yea yea… Angel is cute though," Bridges replied.

"Eww please stop," tears form as I laugh.

She gives me some grace and stops talking about Angel. Instead, we turn to talk about Byron. The soon-to-be eighth grader who was just so sweet…his gentle voice that makes me feel warm inside, his soft curls that seem to turn honey-brown in the sunlight, and his smile that he gives everyone who speaks to him. Byron, the sweet one to all around him.

The eighth grader

Dear Workbook,   May 23, 2004

She said, "really, Byron??… you're into a CHILDD?!?"

I wished I was Catwoman at that moment. I would have hissed and used the bullwhip on Ms. Uppity Up. Byron and I were finally having a conversation, just the two of us when Ms. Uppity Up came around making ugly comments.

Byron yelled back, "are you kidding? This is Angel's kid sister."

Mortified, I look to the side. But first, quickly and swiftly, I glare at her. Byron stops leaning on the wall and straightens up.
Telling me he'll catch me later, he walks off with her.

Why couldn't he just wrap his arms around me? It didn't have to be my non-existent waist, but just my shoulders. He couldn't just yell at Ms. Uppity Up and let her know that: yea, he did find me cute or something? Not that I was so and so's little sister?

Workbook, I'm tired of always feeling like I'm in someone's shadow. If it's not my brother and sisters, it's the "popular girls" of the grade. Let's be honest, they are all skinny...all white...all flirty with the boys. That's not me.

I...have a soft stomach and honey brown skin. And unlike them, I'm quiet. I get tired of teachers telling me to speak up in class, just because I have a soft voice. Is that so bad?

And now, Byron just confirmed he also doesn't see me that way. Thank god for Bridges... if it wasn't for her, Workbook, I'd yell at myself and say all the mean things... like what some of my aunts would say to me on a regular basis.

> **Love Note #4**
>
> You don't need to be like them.
>
> There's a truth in being able to be yourself, without having to be like everybody else.

Unamused

Dear Workbook,   May 25, 2004

I won't forget how she was there for me.

"Amira, relax… you know Angel probably made sure to let every guy know not to get close to you," said Bridges.

Laughing, I tell Bridges, "but he's not even here!"
My big brother may have been popular, but no way did he have the younger kids listening to him.
"No. Byron just isn't into me."

"That's fine though. We're about to go on summer break. When we come back, we'll be in seventh grade. But! We get to go to Playland at the end the year! So, who needs Byron?"

Smiling, I knew she was right. As altar servers, we got to go to Playland for our end of the year celebration. Roller Coasters, cotton candy, hot dogs, the sun. I'll never forget last year laughing and screaming as the roller coaster came down. In polaroid, I'm next to Bridges as Will and Ricky are behind us. "Yea… forget Byron"

I was fine without Byron. I'm ready for Playland.

The Bell

Dear Workbook,   May 31, 2004

I am so ready for the roller coaster rides, the funnel cake with lots of sugar powder on top… Every June.

Every end of the year, we get a trip. All it took was a year of serving the Church. That meant putting on the white robes and the rope belt on our waist. That meant carrying the cross or the candle at the start of Mass. That meant the bell.

All that was required was to serve God.
I can't say I mind my role in the Church.

For the last 2 years, I have served.

Sure, I don't get why I have to wash the Father's hands. All I know is
I have to bring the white bowl, the small white towel (on my arm) and
the glass water pitcher to pour over his hands.

While the Father shows the Church the bread and chalice for
Communion, I get to ring the bell.

The cross-shaped bell: at each end of the cross was a small bell that,
when rung together, called the attention of everyone in the Church.
That was supposed to symbolize that God was present with everyone
and through the Father, at the center of the altar, has turned that bread
and wine into the Body and Blood of our Lord.

Make just enough noise for people to know that today, Mass
happened because of me.

It's a different kind of feeling to know I'm doing something people
appreciate. And. At the end of the year, all us altar servers get to
enjoy a day out of school and have fun at Playland.

That is… if I get permission. After all, grades come first.

Sister, Sister

Dear Workbook,   June 6, 2004

"Listen but don't be heard. Quiet."
"Don't talk out of turn. Hush."
"Do what you are told and don't interrupt."

Do I sound like *mami* yet?

Another day of *mami* telling us to respect our teachers. To listen and do well. But then they ask why we don't ask for help? How or when? If we aren't supposed to interrupt.

Workbook, things I'm tired of hearing:
1 - Do what you are told.
… Okay, but what if I don't understand or get what I'm told to do.

2 - Don't interrupt.
… How am I supposed to be 100% sure if I'm doing this (homework, chores, anything) the way you want?

3 - When I see you and Cristal, I think to myself I've really taught the Fernandez legacy.
… All I can do is roll my eyes and move the little ugly bangs off my face. Sure. I love being grouped in with Catalina, Angel, and Cristal. Workbook, I love my siblings but I'm tired of us being compared to one another.

Do they get that Cristal and I are already twins?! Isn't that enough??

We were awful to some girl. She thought she could say mean things about me. This bratty, thinks-she-is-better-than-everybody child thought I would be left on my own should she make fun of me. Being a twin means I'm never alone. In this instance, I appreciated it. Cristal went hard and went at her! It was great and of course, I wasn't going to leave her alone. That is my twin after all.

But Workbook, *papi* was called to the school. We were sitting in the principal's office when he arrived and Principal K looked like a tomato. She was telling him about all we did to the girl and how she shouldn't be letting us back to school tomorrow.

Cristal and I looked at each other. *Oh shit.*

See Workbook, another thing I'm tired of hearing is…

17

4 - Keep those grades up. The Archdiocese pays for at least half the tuition.
... We know. Lord do we know we are there on scholarship. Every quiz counts. Every grade must be high. Not being in school meant a mark on our record. We couldn't have that. *Papi* is trying to talk to Principal K to say it won't happen again. That we'll apologize. We. We. We.

Workbook, do they get we are TWO people? Do they have to speak for both of us?

We both fought. Got in trouble. Two people, but one meeting. Would it be the same if it was I with a friend not related to me?

I could see the disappointment in their face. I was supposed to be the good girl. I don't act this way.

5 - Study. Don't act this way. Behave.
... Workbook, why is it that they expect Cristal to act out, to be mean, to be louder?
Why can't I be the mean one?
Why can't SHE be the one expected not to act out?
Why do I have to give the right example? To act right.

Why is it that if we both get in trouble, it's only one conversation, and not two?

We each have our own name. Our own body. Our own personality.
Will I always be stuck on repeat playing my song on top of Cristal's?
(Songs meant to be played separately but always played together)

6 - Stay together.
... I love Cristal. Just like how we ended up together in Principal K's office. Workbook, I'd do anything for her. We may fight always. Hate being compared to one another but that's my sister. I know I have to get good grades. I don't want us to lose our scholarship. BUT.

See me.
That's all I want. See me.

Not "me and Cristal" (see her too), because we're already
"the Fernandez Legacy."

Know each of us.

They will know me. They won't forget who I am. Remember
who I am.

Don't confuse me with "Catalina or Angel's sister."
No. I want them to be able to say, "That's Amira Luisa Fernandez."

II: Frozen in Fear

The Big Drop

Dear Workbook,   June 24, 2004

Bridges and I love the sun! Wide eyes, wide smiles! I raised my hands up and I felt the rays touch my *caramelo* skin. I love just closing my eyes and leaning up to the sky. I shrieked out when Connor started tickling me from behind. Oh Workbook, I chased him as soon as he stopped. Luckily for him, there were so many people we had to duck and dodge, that it gave the Monsignor and one of the chaperones (I forget her name) the opportunity to catch us and tell us to stop.

No matter. We waited patiently in line until they handed out the tickets. Like giving a baby candy, all of our eyes lit up. Mine especially, Workbook. It was a beautiful day today and I rode all the rollercoasters!

Super Flight was my favorite! Bridges, Connor, one of Connor's friends and I rode together. AND I got to bring a picture home. My hair was all in Connor's face since I had let it loose and he decided to sit behind me. I showed my parents as soon as I got home, and they just started laughing. I told them how the ride went up a really high hill. I could see most of the park! The fall was the moment the picture was taken, because it's the biggest drop. (But the most fun!) *Mami* gasped as she saw us all screaming and smiling wide-armed in the picture...

The day was so worth it.

Best of all - summer break starts next Tuesday!

Picture Perfect

Dear Workbook   July 10, 2004

We all got into *papi's* car today and drove like thirty minutes to see everyone. And when I say everyone, I mean EVERYONE. Aunts. Uncles. Cousins.

We took a family picture today and I can't believe there's so many of us. Only the kids filled my *tio's* small porch. Angel, Cristal, Catalina, and I are already four. Then there were seven cousins and at least 12 grown-ups there.

We got to sit on the porch with our parents standing on each side.

Picture perfect.

I did good in wearing my denim capri pants and cream blouse. They covered my shoulders and most of my legs. And the bugs didn't get me nearly as much as they got my cousins and siblings. I'm doing my happy dance! The one thing I really don't like about the summer is these bugs. One bite gets to be the size of a quarter with the bump on the top. Itchy, red, and swollen.

Wakala!

I can't lie though Workbook, I even danced a little... Well, what my cousins and I call dancing. Otherwise known as putting on a song that was actually on one of our Kidz Bop CDs and running around in a circle, swinging our arms and making fun of each other.

As we sang happy birthday to my cousin, my aunt brought out the orange cream decorated Dominican cake... *mmm my favorite*!

See, this kind of day is why I was so excited for summer.

Asado

Dear Workbook,   July 23, 2004

I don't want to go to my uncle's tomorrow. I tried to tell *mami* to let me stay home. I know it was fun last time but to see everyone... I don't have the energy inside me to be around everyone right now.

I'm so tired.

Mami let me know that I have no choice, but to go. I can't miss the family summer barbeque. Tio called them to say that he went grocery shopping. Plus, the weather is supposed to be BEAUTIFUL. *Papi* said he's going to bring *la carne* for *el asado*.

Usually Workbook, I'd be all over it without hesitation. *Papi's asado* is my favorite. Dad on the grill is how you know we are having a great summer day.

Some *platano maduro* and sweet potatoes too.

I'm going to go, Workbook. I'll gather up some strength to smile as I greet all of them one by one. Part of me just wants to sit on a chair in the shade. I hope we get there before everyone else, so I don't have to greet each of them one after another after another.

I can't even sleep knowing that we are going tomorrow. It's been so hard to sleep for the last few days...but I'm going to try.

Malcriada

Dear Workbook,   July 25, 2004

I just want to bury my head in my pillow, stay under the covers, and sleep.

Sleep like Sleeping Beauty. At least her rest looked peaceful.

25

Except for last night, I can't seem to close my eyes without having a nightmare. Yesterday didn't go well Workbook. I was *la malcriada*. I tried to be with everyone. I really did... kind of.

We arrived early so it was just my uncle, my aunt, two cousins and us. But I didn't talk much. I didn't play pool with my cousins.

Tia asked what was wrong. I said nothing.

Mami looked at me and said nothing of course, but I could see she wasn't happy with me. The afternoon went on. My uncles would ask me why I wasn't dancing. But Workbook, all I could do was shrug my shoulders. I ate my food, but even then, I was pushing the rice aside. I ate the *ceviche* ever so slowly. I didn't even put sweet potatoes on my plate.

Mami had to pull me aside to tell me to stop being a *malcriada*. But Workbook, what could I do?

I gave them smiles in the beginning.
I hugged them as they came around and said hi.
I ate a lot less than I usually eat, but I ate.
I even laughed at a couple jokes they made.

What else could I do?

Noodles

Dear Workbook,   August 1, 2004

Opening your eyes underwater stings. But it stings even more when it has chlorine in it. That didn't stop me though. I went under the stairs of the pool. At first, it was just to fully be wet. Then the cold could go away faster and I could enjoy the sun shining over the pool.

But Workbook, being underwater felt weightless.

Nothing mattered. My cousins came over to visit and were jumping in… (correction cannonballing in) and playing volleyball in the water with Catalina, Cristal, and Angel. Being underwater while they did it made me feel like life was finally slowing down. I was seeing their bodies in the water moving in slow motion.

I feel like running out of my body every day. The water finally gave me something I haven't felt in weeks. Stillness.

I could've stayed underwater forever. Or at least until Angel threw me a noodle… joking that since I had been under long enough, I needed it to float.

Back up I went.

No Hips

Dear Workbook,   August 11, 2004

It was Angel's birthday today. But when he blew out his candles, I made a wish too.

I wished to feel normal again, Workbook.

Mami had made *aji de gallina*, my favorite chicken dish covered in a creamy yellow pepper sauce, served on rice. I barely ate it.

Even though it wasn't early morning anymore, we sang *Las mañanitas*…Workbook, part of the lyrics says "the day you were born, all the flowers were born."

   El día en que tú naciste, nacieron todas las flores.

I wished to be reborn. I want to shake this feeling of not wanting to be near anyone. I just want a fresh start.

The second after he blew out his candles, we all clapped. I smiled and gave him a hug. Catalina put on some *cumbia* and they all danced together. I actually felt ready to enjoy myself with them again.

I wanted the fresh start, but as soon as the music started playing, my body froze. I'm so confused. I could swing my arms, but my feet and hips didn't want to move. I didn't want anyone getting too close to me, so I danced once and then sat back down.

I don't get why.

Routine

Dear Workbook,   August 20, 2004

Whew! We went Back to School shopping today. New notebooks, pens, sharpeners, erasers, and pencils. I used to love Back to School shopping. The way new crisp loose-leaf sheets feel. The first time that you use a new pen. Summer's coming to an end, but this wasn't the summer I imagined.

I imagined spending more time in the pool, laughing with my siblings and cousins. Helping *mami* and *papi* at work. Going to the park and so much more.

I did go in the water, but not much. I couldn't wear those bikinis or bathing suits. Wearing them made me feel naked. I would just shower and pretend I was underwater again as the water fell over me.

Going to the store was fine. I could spend the morning and afternoon with *mami*. And I would bring a Nancy Drew book with me to see what the new case that needed to be solved was.

I wish she could solve my mystery.

Every afternoon when we left the store, that sensation of running out of my body came back. I look behind my shoulders because I feel someone's eyes. His eyes.

No Workbook, there is no him.

I would run to the closest bakery and pretend to look at the menu. Knowing full well I don't have any money. I would wait a minute or two, then go back to walking home.

Maybe this will be good. Right Workbook? School will get me back into the routine. No more worrying if my shorts or capris are long enough or what T-shirt to wear. No more having to give reasons for not wearing the spaghetti-strapped shirts gifted to me back in June.

No more.

It'll be the ugly uniform again, with the white stockings and bulky black shoes. And when I get home, it'll be homework, not the pool. Back to the books, Workbook.

Maybe I'll go back to normal.

Smallville

Dear Workbook,   September 16, 2004

I can't wait for Smallville to start again! This week has been all re-runs… (which I'm completely okay with).

Tom Welling as Clark Kent is my absolute favorite person to watch on TV. Plus, I feel like him at the beginning of the last season, when he's on Red Kryptonite. But instead of getting involved with a bad guy, I've become someone my family doesn't recognize.

I thought school would get me back to feeling like my nerdy-artsy self again. I'm studious, but every day feels like a daze. I don't talk much in school. It's back to my teachers just seeing me as part of the Fernandez legacy. One thing that I do well now is keeping my nose in a book and out of where it doesn't belong.

Last night, we all rewatched the season finale of Clark finding out the deal Mr. Kent made with Jor-El about bringing Clark home. It was like a bomb went off and Workbook, I feel like that's about to happen to me. Kara came to Clark to reveal the truth and have him fulfill his destiny.

No one knows my secret, Workbook. I feel like unless I tell someone, I won't be able to be the Amira I used to be. Will I have a Kara? Probably not. But as we watched the rerun, I was actually okay being near Cat, Cristal and Angel. Every Wednesday, we would watch Smallville together.

I'm ready to have it back. I'm ready for Amira to be back. Maybe soon…

Knee Jerk

Dear Workbook,   September 30, 2004

I'm ready to tell you my secret Workbook…

I keep thinking of the summer. How I wanted it to be and then what it actually became. Playland did happen - I got stuffed with eating so much junk food. Came home and relaxed. Coming into seventh grade was meant to go smooth. But no.

Today, all I wanted to yell at Cat was "DON'T TOUCH ME".

I jerked my leg away and she just looked at me with a questioning face.

I couldn't look at her.

Big Boss: *Don't look at her.*

If she saw me, she would see the panic in my face. No one could touch me. Tears were starting to form in my eyes, but I blinked them away as fast as I could. If only… If only I could erase the last few weeks… not even. Just that one day.

One of those days, that man…that who-knows-what-he-does uncle, snatched my voice…my innocence. And since then, I've had no desire to smile or laugh. I'm not safe. I don't feel safe. What's the point in being happy? If someone can come and do what he wants to me and not listen to what I want (or don't want). Then what's the point?

It wasn't Cat's fault for all the yelling, screaming or crying. My sister did nothing to harm or betray me. We were just watching a funny scene on TV. All she did was place her hand on my thigh because she was laughing too hard.

I bit my lip, looked at the TV, and slid a few inches away.

No thigh, no hand.

Look Out Lu: *DON'T TOUCH ME. Please.*

I can't do it Workbook. I want to just say what it is that's making me feel this way, but I can't. I can't tell them. I can't even write it out right now.

Innocence snatcher*

Dear Workbook,   October 14, 2004

"Give me one more hug".

I can still see him when I shut my eyes. Mr. Pointy Nose and his who-knows-what-he-does smirky face. I said no, but he still got my hand, placed it, and pressed… Rubbed.

Workbook, I just want to scream it out loud.

31

I gagged inside. To be touched and forced to touch is not something I ever imagined happening to me. I remember asking myself, "How could someone I trust do that? How could someone I was related to do that to me? To his sibling's daughter?"

Doubt.

Look Out Lu: *No one will believe you. Papi borrows his car. I can't be the reason he can't do his job.*

Tears.

Big Boss: *Look away. Don't let him see you cry. Stay calm. You'll be at the store soon.*

It never should have happened. I remember my aunts saying 'hi' as I walked past them that day. Passing by my father has remained a blur. I had to get to the sink. Not because I was going to be sick. (Although I did go into the bathroom to finally let the tears come out) No, I had to get to the sink to wash my hands. That horrible Thursday afternoon in late July was when everything changed.

Clean. Wash it. Again. Anything to stop feeling dirty.

It was like a switch turned off.

Big Boss: *Just get through this.*

I went back to the front of the store to help my dad close the store.

1. Stack the white little boxes of the small earrings.
2. Carry the trays to the safe.
3. Put the covers on top of each set as dad puts the rings and bracelets into the box.
4. Walk to the safe, place it where it belongs.
5. Repeat.

Cheerleader: *One step at a time.*
Big Boss: *Don't show any tears.*
Look Out Lu: *Don't show any panic.*
Big Boss: *Just get through this.*
Look Out Lu: *Get home.*

I can't say I remember much of what my days were like after *that*. What did I call it? I didn't quite have a word for it. All I knew was that I didn't want to be home as much anymore. Anytime Mr. Pointy Nose came around, I did my best to avoid speaking to him (especially whenever I had to get into his car). I can't let myself be in that position again.

Cars. *Shudders*, never again.

Silence.

It all began almost two months ago… maybe three. I don't remember How long it's been anymore.

Love Note #5

Reminders are needed at times to ground us back to the present. What was just read isn't happening at the moment. Instead, look around you. Look for the one thing that makes you feel safe. It can be having a blanket around you or soft music playing.

Where are you? Do you feel safe or comfortable? Can anything be added to ensure that you feel safe as you continue on this journey with me?

Teen Life Skills (TLS)

Dear Workbook,   October 21, 2004

I felt frozen in place, wanting to close my eyes to stop me from seeing it. Hoping to wake up from the nightmare. I remember reading along as Mr. Coffee, my seventh-grade teacher who always had his large cup, read out loud. My eyes got watery. I looked up as I finished reading the definition.

Sexual assault... molestation.

Child molestation... a form of child abuse in which an adult or older adolescent uses a child for sexual stimulation.

No.

Closing my eyes and letting the tears fall, I finally had a word for what happened to me.

I watch every corner and pray that I don't see him. Quiet fills the spaces around me, ever since I stopped talking to people... to my family. Books, books, and more books. Just because I don't feel like myself, doesn't mean I can't get good grades.

I watch my back every day. I run when I think he's nearby.

Say nothing.
Do nothing.
Especially not anything that attracts attention.

It's been a blur...sometimes I forget what day it is.

Then on a Thursday afternoon, I was taken out of my cloud and dropped back into reality.

Another One

Dear Workbook,   October 24, 2004

He didn't get me this time.
He got another.
Look Out Lu: *How could I have let this happen?*

If I had said something sooner...

Workbook, any person can tell you, "It's not your fault." The fight is
to be able to believe it. Not saying anything brought more pain into
my life, into my family's lives (once they knew), and into another
person's life.

I should be buried alive for my silence.

Cops, trains, therapist

Dear Workbook,   October 28, 2004

I was worried that my parents wouldn't even believe me.
Would they still love me?
Would they blame me?

Cops, trains, therapist.

I don't like to cause trouble or stress for them.
They need my uncle, more than I need to tell the truth.
That was the guilt and shame talking.

All this time, I thought the guilt and shame were meant
for me to carry.

Cops, trains, therapist. I thought it would end.

The call to my father's store. It's funny that the first place I went to after it happened to me, was now the first place I called to let my father and Angel know what happened.

Who spoke first? I don't know. I remember hearing Angel repeat the words to my father and Angel being the one to run home. Angel was crying as he hugged me. Angel yelling over the phone telling him that if he ever saw him around here, Angel would kill him.

I was safe, Workbook. I was finally safe.

It was over. I didn't have to hold onto this anymore. Did I?

Cops, trains, therapist. I thought it would end when the truth came out.

But the truth became like a DVD, playing over and over again.
Answering questions, over and over again.
Crying, over and over again.
Taking trains to places, to repeat what was done out loud,
over and over again.
Meeting a therapist to talk through it all, over and over again.

Don't get me wrong. Leticia was nice, tall, and could handle my mom when she wanted to know every single thing we discussed in session. I was safe, but once the truth came out, it's like the tears couldn't stop coming out either.

Imagine a door to your favorite store being opened for the biggest sale of the year. You're in the crowd rushing, pushing and running just to breakthrough. Those were my tears. The little crack in the wall of someone knowing led my tears into taking that small opening and running wild.

Tear after tear, I couldn't make it stop. Over and over again.

Going Under

Dear Workbook,   November 17, 2004

The rest happened in fast forward. Someone else breaking the silence led to me saying it out loud.

"He did it to me too."

Imagine trying to live with yourself when you blame yourself for something someone else did. Something they should have never done. I have been. But I want to live life determined to succeed. No one will tell me I, Amira Luisa, was not smart. To make up for failing to speak up, I will now bring pride to the family. I shall do no other wrong. I will obey, listen, and succeed.

But... I have decided to do it on my own.

Big Boss makes an appearance. *Can't let anyone else get a chance to do the same thing again. Can't let anyone else get a chance to hurt anyone.*

Guilt, anger, shame, and hate were planted that day and since then, I have been **under construction**.

Workbook, childhood sexual abuse is too real. More often than not, it's done by someone the child knows. I, Amira Luisa, knew my attacker. My safety, my innocence, and my smile were snatched. I knew my parents cared for me, loved me. But still, I could not tell them. At least... not until it happened to her. It took someone else to speak so that I could say it too.

Workbook, this feels like what I've been trying to say all summer without realizing it. I lost myself that day. I've been trying to find a way to continue. The days underwater, the stillness was the first time I started to fight the feeling of waiting to die.

I want to breathe again, but I don't know how to. I'm not okay. I'm taking it day by day, the way I know how to. I guess that comes with being under construction. The beauty of it is that it is long-lasting and ever-changing.

One thing is for sure: this is mine.

Love Note #6

Permit yourself to be loved on by others.

Too often do survivors feel they are to blame. They are not. Instead: If at this moment, or any other moment, you feel like you want to isolate yourself, join space with people who make you feel loved. It can be through a phone call, a pressure-free activity (like getting coffee or tea) or sitting and enjoying someone else's company (even in silence).

The Court

Dear Workbook,   February 28, 2005

It's been a while… but the last few months flew by. When it all came out, I was going from one place to another until my mother and I finally got to where we needed to be. Somewhere they weren't saying: "sorry ma'am, but you don't report that here. You have to go to…"

I remember a lady on a steel chair, behind a wooden table, asking me questions.

I can't remember what she looked like.

I do remember the Monday that who-knows-what-he does, Mr. Pointy Nose was sentenced.

Six months.

Who was my lawyer? No idea.

Where did the case take place? No idea.

My parents told me the verdict. Not understanding the courts, my mother told me *"se hizo un trato"* (a deal was made).

Oh, so that's why I didn't see a courtroom, or have to face him.

She saw my face. I don't know if it was one of anger, confusion, or disinterest, but I think it made her want to explain the decision.

"Well *mija*, the lawyer felt we wouldn't have had a case, because there was no evidence."

I nodded. I got it. I stayed quiet, so this is how it goes. The one who he hurt after me was more recent. I wasn't important to the case. Because I waited too long, what he did to me really couldn't be considered important.

Learning that I was not responsible for my uncle's actions, I'm told, will take years. That it was **his actions** that hurt others (and me). That it was **him** who hurt others, not me.

I feel panic when someone gets too close. I want to fight everyone that maybe does one slight thing that annoys me. I have this urge to cry all the time. I'm worried that the next man who enters my life will do it too.

My therapist says those have been me trying to survive. I'm starting to get it now, Workbook.

I, Amira Luisa, have been doing what I had to do to survive.

Love Note #7

There is no "right time" to say: someone hurt me. Someone betrayed my trust. There is no "wrong time".

The only thing one "has to" do is survive.

III: What is Love?

Time to go

March 10, 2009 at 9:28PM

Another day, another application.

One day closer to college. Yeah, it's early but I'm already a junior.

"*Mami*, I want to go to California for college."

Silence. Then the look that makes the little hairs on my neck stand up.

I thought to myself.
Big Boss: *If I get enough scholarships, they can't say no.*

I know that my parents only want what's best for me.

I grew up hearing:
"*La medicina*, this"
"*Doctora*, that"

Cheerleader: *That's not for me mami, sorry. I need to go though.*

College. It's still early, but I know I can't stay in New York.

Too much history.
Too much pain.
Too much noise.

STOP
Please. Just make the noise stop.

In my head, the memory is screaming on repeat.

I can't stay in the same house, where I shed so many tears...so much anguish. Where I felt so much rage. Where I felt like, brick by brick, I was being anchored down. So much so, that it was like I was being buried alive.

It was time to go.

36K
June 26, 2009 at 10:28PM

Standing in a graduation crowd, I stood in shock.

People that I didn't know were clapping…for me?
*Myself and two other peers to be exact.

What was happening? Why were they clapping? It wasn't my graduation.

I saw the presentation slide announcing the scholarship recipients for incoming high school seniors.

- Amira Luisa Fer…

Woah.

Big Boss: *Not bad Amira. It's actually possible to get away now. What are we up to? 32… $36,000 for four years?*

Not. BAD.

Standing tall, I looked at my other two peers. We were all in different sections of the crowd. They were as stunned as me. We just raised our hands and cheered for each other from afar.

Why Go
June 28, 2009 at 11:37 PM

Look Out Lu: *I need to get away.*
Big Boss: *I need to leave.*

44

Cheerleader: *To start new, fresh.*

Run. Run and don't stop.

Cheerleader: *Run so you can breathe again. So, the weight of your heart can move, so your heart can pump normally again.*

Big Boss: *Normal. HA! What is that?*

I'm thinking of two days ago. It felt unreal to be told I, as a junior, had enough money to go away for college. I did it. I can leave! I can go upstate!

I can't stay in the city. Not after everything that's happened. I keep thinking of how *mami* wants me to be a doctor, but it's not what I want. I need room to breathe. Also, the schools I'm looking at are not for medicine. It feels like the only promise to *mami* I do feel comfortable making is to at least become a professional.

Then I'd have something that no one could take away from me.
My education.
My life.

I'm struggling, though. How do I explain that, the thought of staying in the city and commuting everywhere in the trains or buses, makes me feel like I'm locked in a closet with creepy crawlers climbing everywhere?

I'm looking for a school that offers alternative classes, a dorm and space. Maybe a school where I can see the stars at night? Where I can breathe fresh air, close my eyes and sleep easy. A place that I can just be me. Not someone's twin or little sister.

I love my parents. They want what's best for me. But I know their plans and their way is not mine. It's not for me. They raised me to recognize what is meant for me. They built me up to where I could now say, "I hear you, but no." "Thank you, but I have to figure this one out on my own."

I'm creating a space where I can just be me.

Cheerleader: *Yes. Me. Oh, to find out what that means.*

Where I could thrive.

Big Boss: *Whatever that looks like.*

I'll make something of myself wherever I go. I'll make them proud of me. Even when a Mr. Sly Guy or a Mr. Heart did come rolling around in my life, threatening to take *mis ganas de luchar* away.

Sly Guy*
                    July 2, 2009 at 11:17 PM

I remember his caramel skin, his short-military-but-not-military haircut. But most of all, I remember his pinkish, full, half smiling, half smirking lips. The brown eyes that looked at me like how a little kid looks at cake.

He was dangerous. The kind of dangerous where what I thought were butterflies in my stomach should have been fire alarm bells. My excuse? … I was a freshman and I didn't know any better.

I would say Sly Guy was the person that I could never forget.

His image - embedded in my memories.

At 14, he made me laugh harder than any time since before I was 12.

Two years.

The kind of laugh that hurt my stomach; where it would sound like me gasping for air. I'd laugh so much, it hurt.

The way he made me blush … he would notice me when I did my best to be invisible. I'd use my books to hide my face. He would come around smiling, giving me the look that said, I see you.

I remember when he put himself next to Daniella at the same time that I took her picture.

"Now you can have a picture of the both of us."

Turning red, I would look away.

Him and his purple t-shirt. His smile.

To him, I say "Thank you" for making me smile and blush in the moment… Even for the multiple moments of hurt that came in the months after the picture.

Love Note #8

Take some time to breathe. It's easy to say "I should have known this was going to happen" after the fact. You only knew what you knew in the moment.

Shame. Self-hate. Self-blame. No one is responsible for what another person does, except the person that does it.

Take a moment to sit with a pet or imagine the voice or face of someone or someplace that you love.
1. If you find yourself feeling upset or distressed while reading, bring them forth physically or mentally.
    a. Remember why you chose them
    b. Focus on what their characteristics are. Concentrate on the feelings THEY (not the section) brings up for you.

I hated him for a long time. The way that smirk-smile became the one to take mine away. Again.

He asked if I was ready. Confused, I said ok. I didn't know what he was talking about, but I didn't want to look dumb in front of him. I didn't ask any questions. Two years ago, everything changed. Again.

His hand went to the top button of my jeans. I pulled my hands up to push him off and said "stop". It was like the little person in my brain was finally ringing the bell, trying to keep the fire from spreading.

"This isn't a good idea. Let's stop. Someone could come in."

Because who would want things to go further in a dark, dirty, old college locker room?

I didn't. I didn't want to have sex.

But at 15, I didn't want to be 'uncool.' And it seemed like Sly Guy was the guy that every girl wanted. The one every guy wanted as a friend. He said, "c'mon. You said yes already… it'll be fun."

I said "fine."

I had changed my mind. No one told me that I could. He told me that I couldn't.

Cheerleader: *Look at the ceiling. How many lines are up there?*
Big Boss: *Don't make a noise.*
Look Out Lu: *Don't yell. Don't cry.*

Most importantly though, Amira, don't feel. Flip the switch.

Off.

Shortly after, I hoped it would be over and it was. Thankfully, he didn't last very long.

Sly Guy finished and I put my jeans back on and left. Did he know that I cried on the train ride home that day? I called Bridges and told her my virginity was gone.

Look Out Lu: *You mean the one thing society tells girls to keep but not keep. Damned if you do, damned if you don't.*

Snapping back to reality, I had decided that I wouldn't let her hear me cry. Telling her what happened was just too risky.

The people on the train with me saw though.

She was shrieking, excited, wanting to know how it was.
I said nothing. I feigned excitement.
I wondered...

Look Out Lu: *Did the people on the train hear me? Do they know?*
Big Boss: *What do they think?*
Look Out Lu: *Did they even care?... Probably not.*

Little did I know, that would be the first of (what seems like) hundreds of times that Sly Guy would be the reason I cried on trains for months.

Love Note #9

You can say no at any time. You are allowed to change your mind. In and beyond this book, you can say no at any time.

To survivors: it's not your fault. You are here now. You are not alone.

Take a deep breath. Use any of your five senses that can support you in moving through any distress you feel. It can look like: 1. putting your hands in water (warm? cold?) 2. listening to a song that makes you feel at ease 3. Breathing (slow) 4. Eat or drink (sweet? salty?) 5. A short walk (how're your feet feeling? slow?)

Take care of yourself as necessary. This is a journey; go at your own speed.

Like a robot*
July 6, 2009 at 11:48 PM

Go to school. Afterschool. Take the train home. But Him? He didn't make it quite so simple.

The next time, it wasn't a locker room. At least the first time was private.

Like a robot, I followed him. All his commands. No longer protesting. On my knees when He wanted me to be.

I hated Sly Guy.

I hated Him because He made me believe that's what sex was. That doing as I was told, was what I had to do.

I hated Sly Guy.

Instead of a smile, His face brought a cloud over me. Instead of a smile, a line would form. My blank stare.

Look Out Lu would say, *Oh no! Not again!* in my head.

Seeing Him meant being on my knees again, at yet another train station.

The letter or number train or train station didn't matter. It's like He knew all the cracks that He could take me into (or in these cases, have me take him). In these disgusting, dark, but still-close-enough-for-people-to-find-us places, He had all the control. He'd push me down and hold me in place. And I did as I was commanded.

I would hear the tracks roar and the wind from the train get closer. It was all I could do, to make sure they couldn't see my face as the train went by. I prayed with all my might, that we wouldn't get caught. Yes, getting caught would have brought an end to those Robot months. BUT...

The embarrassment. The shame. It would be too much. It's not like He had a gun on me "forcing" me. What would I say when they yelled: "What are you doing here?!" No.

I couldn't bring shame to my family like that. Not again. The humiliation? I couldn't go through that. I mean, no one could find out.

Sly Guy was the kind of guy that could make anyone believe it's what I wanted. *"I was the one after him."* Mr. Pointy Nose did the same thing. *"She seduced me."* He would also say things that would make me believe it was consensual. So how could I tell anyone I really didn't want to be on my knees? I couldn't.

The conniving, manipulative, egotistical jerk had a way of silencing the cry and the scream and the roar that laid inside of me.

No, I would just do as I'm told.

It wouldn't be until I was almost 17 that I found out, "You can definitely change your mind about sex or that you don't have to do it if you don't want to." I didn't see it as non-consensual. I didn't tell anyone that I didn't want it. I could never gather the courage to say the words.

Mr. Porcupine Hair
July 9, 2009 at 12:48 AM

He had no idea. My closest friend. The one who always made me feel safe. The one who went to school with me. The one who would take the train home with me. He had NO IDEA.

I mean. How could he? He thought that I liked spending time with Sly Guy.

And what else could he think? I never said anything. I never uttered a word about what He had me doing.

There's the shame and embarrassment again. I didn't want him to think I was a slut. Because who in their right mind would give someone oral sex in a train station.

Me. Was I in the right mind though?

It was a Thursday evening. It was always a Thursday evening. I asked him. I told Mr. Porcupine Hair: "I'm going to take the train home with you (so don't leave without me)."

I told him without telling him. It wasn't enough.

I tried to hide from Him, but he went looking for me. And Mr. Porcupine Hair didn't know. So, when Sly Guy asked him, "Hey, where's Amira Luisa?" He told Him.

Like a robot, I went.

I hated Sly Guy.

But. Like my dad would always say. *"No ganastes el juego pero ganastes experiencia."*

Love Note #10

To the family and friends of survivors: it's not on you. You don't have to have the right words, just be there. Be present if you can be. If at this moment, you remember a survivor, this section isn't meant to make you feel guilty. Instead, it's meant to be honest about a struggle many are asked about - the Why didn't you say anything? I offer that it's not the easiest thing to do when you are battling yourself and the voices of your thoughts pulling you in all directions.

To readers: Be kind to yourself and others. If someone asks for help, it shows how much you mean to them that they felt they could go to you for support. Support can take multiple forms. Talking to them, supporting them in connecting them to resources, going to a clinic or hospital if wanted, taking them to a space they want to be in, being present fully with them.

To survivors reading: take a minute to show yourself some love. Drink your favorite beverage. Repeat words of affirmations to yourself. Give yourself some grace.

It's okay to have done what was needed in the moment with what was known. Amira shows she did what she needed to do in the moment with what she knew she could do.

You didn't win the game, but you gained experience*
July 14, 2009 at 12:57 AM

No ganastes el juego pero ganastes experiencia.

After every game ended, *Papi* would say it.

Every basketball game. Every softball game. Every tennis game.

Angel or any cousin would play, it would end and all I could do was
hear it and roll my eyes. Every. Single. Time.

If I remember correctly, I heard it at least once a week from the time I
was nine, until I was thirteen.

This phrase is why I can say 'Thank You' to Sly Guy.

Sly Guy taught me that love comes with pain. Two years ago, at 15, I
believed that following commands like a robot was what being in love
meant. He could take what He wanted, with no regard for me, my
body, or my feelings. And that was love.

"They're birthday punches. Plus one for good luck," He said.

That's what he called the bruises that he left on my arm on my 15th
birthday (my *quinceañera*). They turned a shade between red and
purple so quickly that for a moment, I thought He was using a
baseball bat. With every punch, He saw me close my eyes to stop the
tears. I bit my lower lip so that no one could hear me scream. And He
just laughed and smiled.

During my party, I used my dress wrap to hide them from my family
and the pictures. I mean, if there were no pictures, then there was no
proof. And no proof means that it didn't happen. Right? And all I had
to do was hide the pain and try not to move my arm.

I just wanted to take my brain out of my head and wipe my memory clean like a computer. Just like new. Not just for the train stations or the birthday, but so much more. Like the traffic incident.

MickeySmiles yelled, "let her go!" And grabbed me before I was hit.

And He just laughed like a maniac as MickeySmiles pushed Him off of me. It was like my soul, my voice, and my fight was trapped inside my body. And I was there, frozen, watching myself being grabbed and led into oncoming traffic. How did any of that make sense?

I asked myself: Why? Why did I let it happen? Why didn't I fight back? I resisted Him, but He wore me out. He had some pounds and inches on me, but why did I give up?

I thank Sly Guy. (not literally)

I believed that love comes with pain. Should I want something, too bad. I don't get to have it. I was a little girl that saw what she thought was cake but could never have it.

M. Scott Peck said, "Love is as love does. Love is an act of will- namely, both an intention and an action. Will also implies choice. We do not have to love. We choose to love."

I didn't know or understand that back then. I thought I was choosing love.

Love
  -   to do anything for him.
  -   to not fight him when he convinced me to have sex otherwise.
  -   to go with it even when he knew I wanted to say no.

Love was giving. Giving everything until the tank was Empty. And only when it actually reached Empty, could I finally walk away. And for me, Empty was when I was prepared to die.

I remember the moment. It was in one of those train stations. I said,

"No. I don't want to anymore." I was like a shaken soda bottle, about to be opened. All the bubbles rising, about to explode.

He took me by my wrists, and I thought he was gonna slam my head on the metal train tracks. But no... he made my hands feel his 16-year-old body as if that was really supposed to change my mind.

"You sure...?" he said.

I nodded.

Big Boss: *100 percent sure!*

Everything went into fast forward. The train came seconds later, and I went into the corner of the first car and started hyperventilating.

It was over. I did it. I said no.

I, Amira Luisa, FINALLY said no.

It took time to realize what I was saying no to. How my body, my mind, and my heart were saying no to any person trying to get close to me after what happened with Sly Guy.

I continued to be the straight-A student that I had been.
The smart one. The nice one. The shy one...
at least until Mr. Heart came around.

Mr. Heart

July 18, 2009 at 1:28 AM

It began with doubts. I remembered questioning whether or not he really liked me, or only went out with me because he knew that I liked him (which would be his own issues to deal with). My thing was the level of insecurity and mistrust that I felt. I'd panic thinking he didn't really like me. Or that I was just convenient.

What would I have to do for him?

He was kind. And corny. The kind of corny, that I would roll my eyes at. But I'd smile because he was a joy to be around. I remember telling him, "I love you."

Lord, what did that mean?

Safety. Peace. Security.

Four months in and he had given me space to just be me. He hadn't forced me to do anything that I didn't want to do. He understood. And he was patient... really patient. We laughed. We went to the movies.

(We went to a lot of movies!)

At least in those first few months, being with him was easy. Whenever we wanted to laugh, we'd go back to the song that was in the first movie we saw as a couple. But the doubt, the questions, the jealousy, the arguments, and those thoughts started.

The thoughts.

Big Boss appears on my shoulder and sarcastically would say, *"you remember those wonderful thoughts he had?"*

The "oh this girl was cute... oh I was thinking about such and such looking pretty today"

Bless his soul that he had not gone up and kissed someone.

He was honest, though. EVERY. SINGLE. DAY.

I understood that being in high school, during puberty, our hormones were on a thousand, but DAMN.

I hoped for just one day. ONE. DAY. That I wouldn't have to get a text message, telling me: "I'm sorry babe, it happened again."

Was I not enough?

I, Amira Luisa, understood he was a guy. Guys look. I look. I have eyes to recognize when someone is funny, cute, charming or all of the above. But I didn't go telling him about it. Why?

I already believed that I had to do things to keep him. And not just sexual things. If we fought, somehow it was my fault.

I made mistakes. I was by no means perfect. I, however, did nothing to deserve him making me feel ugly, unworthy, or just not pretty enough. Enough that he wouldn't find someone else attractive almost every day that we didn't see each other.

Then again, I always wondered if he resented me for having him wait… 11 months.

He was patient. Really patient.

I would tell him that I DID NOT want his first time to be with me. How could I be worthy enough to be his first? In those times, I felt worthless.

He knew about Sly Guy, but not Sly Guy's name
… not until much later.

Everyone in school would always say: "you never forget your first."

They were right. I found it impossible to forget Sly Guy. No matter how hard I tried, I phrased it as *he'll always be attached to me, somehow, to one part of my story.*

Mr. Heart taught me that's all it was --- just one part.

Train Rides
July 22, 2009 at 12:26 AM

Mr. Heart lived an hour and a half away from me. Maybe more. Every weekend before classes (you know because we were nerds), he would pick me up at home. Then we would travel in the terrifying trains for

another hour.

The trains were not terrifying. They were not the reason I wanted to jump out of my skin and cry every time men surrounded me during rush hour. Or run out every time they become packed. I couldn't breathe because the panic was too much. The fear that I would be touched or forced to do something I didn't want to do. I was thinking of Sly Guy or Mr. Pointy Nose. After all, they shaped how I viewed men back then.

Ugly, scary enforcers of sexual desires. It wouldn't matter if I said no. What I wanted, in the end, wouldn't be enough to stop an attack. All I was good for after all was "for them to get off."

Mr. Heart held me a little tighter when I felt the urge to run.

"I got you," he would say. "It's okay."

He was the one that brought me back into my body. When my insides were telling me: *RUN. GET OUT. IT'S GOING TO HAPPEN AGAIN,* he was the voice telling me "You are safe now. You are not alone. Nothing bad is happening right now."

Hugs began to feel safe again. I could feel not only my arms relax around him, but my heart.

I thank Mr. Heart and also say, "I'm sorry. I shouldn't have created that kind of pressure on you to make me feel safe. I loved you for it, though, because you did it without being asked. You somehow knew that I needed you and you showed up."

La Puerta
(The Door)

August 20, 2009 at 2:42 AM

Mr. Heart showed me that love had a different door. A door where two people could walk through, care for each other (argued at times, yes), and try to look out for one another. A door that even when we argued, and others saw (and were concerned), we could always come back to understanding each other.

But what happens when those arguments grow so unhealthy, that neither of us is happy? *La General* happens.

La General
(The General)

August 20, 2009 at 3:12 AM

"Go talk to someone"

Mr. Heart and I looked at each other with the face of *can I come up with a reason why I can't?*

Who wants to talk about how parents have abandoned us, people have harmed us, and all we were trying to do was make someone see that WE were ENOUGH?

We were enough and *La General* saw us. *La General* was the one who meant business, the one people saw and knew they couldn't mess with her. The person who cared enough to tell people what they NEEDED to hear, not what they WANTED to hear. The one leader in the playground everyone knew to listen to when she spoke.

We were enough and *La General* saw us.

Maybe she didn't have time to deal with our drama, but she didn't ignore us. She saw us and told us talking to someone might help. This was love.

It helped, at least for me. Now almost two years later, three maybe, and it's like the window was broken to finally let air in.

"Amira, if you didn't want to, you had every right to say no or change your mind."

Broken Window*
                    October 8, 2009 at 12:58 AM

Initially, I wanted to run.

Look Out Lu with our face full of dread said, *I let it happen again.*

Big Boss: *No. It wasn't rape because in the end we agreed to it. It wasn't rape because it happened more than once. It wasn't rape because we didn't tell anyone. We didn't say anything, again.*
  ...
Big Boss: *It wasn't rape.*

It's hard to say it was.

I, Amira Luisa, can recognize that I didn't want it. On certain days, I know I've gone through violence, intimate partner violence, assault. But on other days, it's still hard for me to say Sly Guy made me do something against my will, something I did not want to do.

The air was filled with compassion though. Understanding - for the fear and panic that all men were out to get me. Love - that I deserve to breathe.

I, Amira Luisa, am deserving of a relationship, where I could be myself without the fear that I wasn't enough. Without having to try and prove I was worthy at every step. And La General gave me the opportunity to see this, by offering that we could go talk to someone.

Love Note #13

Both will exist. The awareness of things that should have never happened did and also finding it difficult to say and accept that they did - is part of the process. Let it come as it does. Show kindness to others, not because you do (or do not) know their story but because we all may have to face a moment in our lives where it may be difficult to accept it - whatever that "it" may be.

Stomp on it... like a duck
                    January 15, 2010 at 2:26 AM

Not everyone could be *La General.* Love, however, was also *La Comandante* (the commander). This was the woman with the "I'm-tall-everyone-is-just-taller" personality. But with an attitude that commands, like when a judge walks into their courtroom. Everyone would stop, look, listen, rise and sit when told to.

"Things will happen…and they will weigh on you. Don't let them."

Everyone knew her, but Mr. Heart and I had only known her a few months. She was showing us (me) that life will happen. She reminded us (me), that we can. We can make it and we can push through, because life will happen.

Life would life. Life would try and knock us down, but we could "shake it off and stomp on it like a duck."

She then proceeded to show us how a duck would walk.
La Comandante smiled.

Oh, how I loved and appreciated her.

Was she preparing us for what was to come?

She was, because life happens.

Caught up
                    March 24, 2010 at 12:31 AM

"Don't go to college with a boyfriend."

Our relationship was a roller coaster. The thoughts, the doubt, the tears. And then…the cops.

We broke up one time for a couple of weeks. I dated, then went back to him (but not officially).

Big Boss: *You mean the going back where we act and do things as a couple but aren't. (rolls eyes)*
Look Out Lu: *Yea. That.*

He got sick of it. We fought again. I cried. I tried to walk past him. He blocked my way. I backed away as his voice got as loud as the roar of the oncoming trains.

Cops: "Miss, did he put his hands on you?"

"NO."

Look Out Lu: *No. Nothing else can happen.*

Now I was not only upset but I was worried for his safety.

"No officer. We were just arguing. He has never laid a hand on me. Thank you."

We were so caught up on one another, that I knew that if we went to college as a couple, we would never establish ourselves as individuals. The words of advice given to me by my sister's best friend echoed in my head. "Don't go to college with a boyfriend." *Was this why?*

I feared that I would never establish myself because I'd be tied to him. He would never ask me to do so, but I would want to - to show that I was loyal to him. Here I am, approaching graduation and I have this fear, that he would leave me behind or believe that I was no longer what he wanted. Why? Insecurities.

He never forgave me. He never forgave me for breaking his heart. And who could blame him? Not me. I'm still caught up, but I broke up with him, just to not be in a relationship at school.

Sly Guy taught me to question love. To believe that love was painful and knew no boundaries and would always cost me more than it could ever give back.

Mr. Heart might've confused me, but he restarted my heart. He taught me how to open the windows, pull back the gate after a lockdown. He made hugs feel safe again. But he also made me think that love meant constantly questioning if I was good enough. Was I selfish to leave?

Love, I saw, was also *La General* and *La Comandante.* Tell it how it is, no funny business, get down to business, stay hungry kind of love. The 'fight for your dreams, because I believe in you' kind of love.

The 'I love you and I will push you to believe in yourself and your capabilities' kind of love.

Then there's the love that has always been by my side.

Mami, thank you for believing in me. *Papi*, thank you for choosing us. Above all, thank you both for dreaming for me when I didn't know I was deserving of dreaming for myself. For believing in my abilities. In me. Thank you for letting me live my dream to figure out this thing we call life on my own. I know you were scared; I was too.

Caught up or not, I went on living…

IV: Yes. Right?

Unsalted

October 12, 2010 at 1:11 AM

This isn't what I thought it would be like…

In the center of the room is the salad bar. To the left is the Chinese food station, to the right the grilled food station, and the middle the pizza and cheese fries station.

All I want is *mami's* food, my bed… some sleep.

How funny. I went through looking at *mami's* disappointed face in April for this. I cried in my room after Angel asked, "why would you go and get yourself into debt when there are colleges you could commute to?" I said goodbye to my friends in August when we went to the park days before I flew away for college. Cut a cake when those friends surprised me at home the night before I left.

I'm still getting calls from uncles and aunts telling me to think about my family, how much it hurts them for me to have left. To get it from aunts and uncles living by us is one thing but for those who don't, who live 6 to 9,000 kilometers away to call and tell me it…
I have to push through.

I have two more midterms. After that maybe… maybe I'll have some time to relax. To paint. To write. Spend time with friends (although we all are going through the struggle right now). To call my parents. To sleep. To eat.

To eat… I can't wait to have some of *mami's arroz verde*.
My mouth waters at the thought. Anything of *mami's* would be better than this unsalted rice on my plate.

Crumbs

Who knew it could take so long to get home?

The first time, it was a direct, less-than-two-hour plane ride. Now? Two planes and having to go south first, then north.

On top of that…getting caught in the rain on my way to the airport, so I got to sit in wet clothes. I could see the wet strains of hair in my face, while I was scrunching my lips to the side as I took a selfie for my siblings.

A mess.

The first semester is over.

Finals are done and I have nothing else to worry about but spending time with my family. I looked at the last picture before my selfie…it was five girls around a small table-sized Christmas tree. We made it. Together. One down, seven to go. So, I guess I'm gonna just rest my head on this seat and close my eyes until they announce my plane is arriving.

The sky is gray out the window. It's like the world is mocking me because I went away to college. Now, I can't wait to go home. Instead of calling *mami* every other day or once a week, I can see her every morning. At least for a couple of weeks. Who would have thought that me going away would bring me closer to them?

It's like we're following cookie crumbs on a path to being a closer family unit. And it doesn't matter that this semester hasn't gone as expected. Friends were made. I kind of got used to not living at home and going to school out of state. College classes are **killer** - I'm worried about what my parents are going to say about me not getting A's in class.

Oh, but there's relief… because I know my family misses me as much as I miss them.

And… they just announced that my plane is here. Time to go home.

Showers

March 15, 2011 at 1:37 AM

Running to the church-looking building, Keila and I screamed as we saw the lightning miss the tree to our left by a couple of feet. We go up the stairs and take cover over under the overhang.

Keila turned to me once we were safe. "I didn't know you could run so fast!"

Shaking my head, I said, "neither did I."

Laughing, I told her I love a good rainstorm, but I prefer to not have my laptop with me.

There's something about the pouring rain that feels like everything is being washed away. Fears, worries, doubts…

The water that was hitting my face, I could usually look up to the sky and welcome it with a wide smile and open arms. It reminds me of when *mami* goes specifically out in the pouring rain to feel her feet being washed as she also cleans the back part of the house.

In this case, I didn't need my laptop to have water damage while I tried to finish the fifteen-page midterm paper. I was walking home from the library because I was basically done. I was leaving tomorrow just for final edits.

The last two months have been chaotic enough. I don't need anything else to go wrong. From five to two sticking together… I guess drama doesn't just miraculously end in high school. I, however, choose not to get caught up with it. The three showed they are different from

Sara and me and there's nothing wrong with it, but our friendship was more arguments than fun times because of our different personalities.

For me

September 20, 2011 at 1:31 AM

In the thing that we call life, there is work. File papers. Create a curriculum. I, Amira Luisa, could work. Everyone who knew me knew I worked in what mattered to me.

Not a straight-A college student. But a hard worker? yes.

HELL yes

I've made sure to focus more on what matters during these last six months. As much as I didn't expect to get caught up with the drama, partying, and boys when I got to college, I did. Where did that leave me? In academic probation. Time to go back to the Amira I used to be. Instead of getting good grades because our scholarship requires it, I do it because I can do better than academic probation.

My love for work is a mountain that could never be broken, only trailed.

It's time to get back to it which is why I went in this second year ready to say what I want to do.

"I want to work with women, children, and families impacted by domestic and sexual violence"

"It's possible but not always done with our program Amira"

"I'll be the one to continue it"

"I'll see what and who we can partner with to get you that internship"

Thank you.

I've made it this far. States away from home, I can focus on the center I want to create. Maybe work with? Not sure.

One thing is for certain - I'm not taking for granted having a program help me find work while in school. I'm a sophomore now. This is my chance to really focus on supporting people who have been through this. What I've been through.

Some Days
October 11, 2011 at 12:17 AM

Every morning, three times a week, I smile. I don't have to go to class. I get to walk into town and work alongside great people.

I'm usually at my desk when I hear the door chime. Sometimes it's two or three families. Other times, it's ten to fifteen women coming in a day. One social worker takes a family, another one takes a woman who comes on her own. Some are filing for orders of protection; some have family court cases. No case is the same. Each of them has their own story.

The people that come in are saying enough to the violence and are reaching out. I walk over to Catherine to let her know when I'm done.

She's taught me what to do, has taken me "under her wing". For a supervisor, I thought she would be intimidating. But that's just how I feel about my elders. They tell me what to do, no questions asked. On the other hand, Catherine asks **me** if I have questions. She knows this is the work I want to be doing and wants to teach me.

This work isn't about me (even if I've been through similar situations). It's what I see when I get there… I see strength, love, and power step into the office every time I am there. Hand in hand, women, children, families walking in. It seems like I can see their breaths fill them up with courage, fight, the will to keep going.

I'm not alone. All around me, individuals have been saying enough.

Others "no more". I know why this cause is important to me and part of being in a small-town organization makes me feel less alone surrounded by survivors - resilient and brave. I also feel like a hypocrite.

How can I be there if I also don't have the ability inside me to say no more? Why? Because years have passed. There is no evidence. No proof. Who would believe me?

Love Note #14

You can feel okay some days. Other days you may question yourself more or doubt your abilities. If right now, you feel like things are going the way they should be, great! Keep your head up, keep going. If right now, you are experiencing feelings of discomfort, sadness, overwhelmed, nervous, that is okay. I ask you to join me in practicing this tool.

To call us to attention to where we are and where we want to be: picture yourself at a different moment where you have felt more at peace, relaxed or at ease. Notice what is around you. Who is around you? Are there any particular sounds or colors present? A song, quote, or food? Are you in a specific setting?

Before continuing, allow yourself to be in that picture. Take a deep breath and keep going when you are ready.

Forró

January 19, 2012 at 2:49 AM

I thought I had won the opportunity of a lifetime. To go visit, study, and live (for a month) in a different country. Two months ago, I got the news that I was accepted. I just needed to pay half, since I qualified for aid and my visa. I was going to Brazil!

74

Now, I'm here. Everyone was smiling, dancing to *forró*. *Minha mãe (my [host] mom)* was laughing, smiling, having the time of her life next to me. All it took was for one man... one drunk, older man to get too close to me.

Here I was, in beautiful Brazil and the nightmare came back. My body's lockdown system began. It's like what you see in the movies – gates closing, windows shutting, no one being able to go in or out.

I don't understand why this is happening again. I just want to go back to the States. I want to be at home. My body can't stop shaking. One of the girls from the program had made plans for us to all go out but I couldn't anymore. It's like I'm stricken with fear and I can't move past it. I stayed with *minha mãe* tonight and watched tv. She tried to make me feel better. Without asking too many questions, she knew the incident of the man getting too close to me struck me. It's why she pulled me away from him. I froze. Again. He just wanted to dance but I didn't like his arms on my waist.

I reached out to Mr. Heart. After months of not speaking and some explaining as to why I was reaching out, I received a response to my text messages. He reminded me – just one part of my story.

"Breathe, Amira Luisa. You are okay."

Hollywood*
February 12, 2012 at 12:15 AM

I returned... but I wasn't okay. Returning from Brazil, I was told. I heard what happened.

Hollywood had the honey, golden-brown curls that I used to love playing with. Arms that opened so wide to give me the biggest bear hug on earth. When I was in high school, Hollywood was my friend. He, the one who was soft, gentle, and loving. The person who helped me believe good men existed.

75

My loving "teddy bear", that loving friend, went Hollywood once we got to college.

Who knew him? Not me.

I did not know him. Not I. Especially, when the story was spoken … He did not listen to someone's- No.

But why was I surprised? He always got what he wanted. Like the night he said he just wanted to study. The night he was dishonest. The night he chose to do things I had no say in.

I was so disappointed more so because of what happened after the news.

Division.

"He didn't do it."
But he did. Who were we to question someone who came forward to
     say her no was not listened to?

"They just want to kick out another brown student."
Maybe so, but he didn't listen.

He didn't listen and it was that moment I realized. It was more important to listen, not get caught up in the "proof." They mattered. Above all else, they mattered.

I've walked out of classrooms because a professor (yes, a professor) had the audacity to question a charge that was made against a male celebrity. Asking what proof did the woman have against him to show she said no? I thought I was in one of those horrible tv ads that show the questions that are usually asked challenging a survivor.

- What were you wearing?
- Did you kiss them before? Were you flirting?
- Why did you meet them for dinner?

It didn't matter. It doesn't matter. What matters is that their No, their voice, was not listened to. What they are saying now matters. Sometimes, our voice is speaking in nonverbals. So much can be said by not moving or speaking. Just like some are quick to react when threatened, others freeze. Some may even try to run. All we have to do is listen. Listen closely. Watch and notice changes.

I'd be lying if I said I wasn't disappointed in Hollywood. Just like I was that day with my professor.

Love Note #15

It's not easy to hear about people we know being accused of something terrible. Oftentimes there is a rift among those who believe vs. don't believe that the person they know is being accused. It's natural to not want to believe the worst in someone. It's just as important to not negate the experience of a survivor. It takes a lot to come forward. To battle with *will they believe me, what will they do to me, will I be supported, etc.*

Take a minute. If at any point you were not believed about something you did, went through, experienced or witnessed:

I see you.
I hear you.
I believe you.

Goodbye*

March 22, 2012 at 2:57 AM

We all have a story. Mine has been focused on trying to find my way through life trying to feel even the least bit safe. Some around me are the first in their families to go to college. However, others feel

77

burdened by the expectations of their families that they tried to leave this world. Last week… I got to see what that can lead to.

"Hey Amira, look what Loren just sent me"

Looking at her phone, certain words made the dread come back, my blood rushing down my face as if I was turning pale. "… I just want to thank you… remember me… please tell them… I love them…"

"When did she send this to you?"
"A few minutes ago, why?"
"We need to go. NOW"

Three of us grabbed our coats and hats. I'm not sure I remember how we got to Loren's place. I remember the dark night surrounding us, the stars staring back at us, the scenery that made me remember peace was now screaming RUN. GO! NOW! HURRY!

I didn't go inside. I didn't go inside because Sara and Keila went in. After all, they were her sisters. They got the messages. Fast forward a few seconds later, they were banging on her room.

I will never forget… I will never forget holding Sara as she cried because she didn't understand. All I could say was "we got here. We got here just in time. Loren was still able to open the door. You were here, you were there to keep her awake while the ambulance came… You may not always understand, but just know you were there for her."

I don't know if what I said was right, but it's what came out. I remember the feeling of being ready to die. Everything I went through with Sly Guy, just to say no, I was scared. I didn't know how he would react so as I got ready to say no, I also felt the need to be okay with dying. I can't imagine what it would have been like for my family to find out I was killed or if I had jumped into the train tracks. What I knew was Sara needed me. That night, in finding Loren having taken the number of pills she did, Sara needed me. We don't know what Loren was going through, or what's been going through in her mind, what she's kept to herself. I just know now, we need to check in more.

I can't say I know why Loren made the attempt she made. What I can say is this moment has been my wake-up call.

The "Get help. Don't go through this alone. Let others in. Talk to someone; it's okay to go back to therapy" wake up call.

Eventually. Eventually, I will. I just don't know if I'm ready yet.

Almost
June 23, 2012 at 11:39 PM

I gathered up some strength today...to speak.

Looking at *mami* and *papi* from across the table, I said:
"I bought a one-way ticket back home at the end of March."

Scrunching up their faces, they both look at me confused.

No questions asked. They were waiting for me to continue. I felt like my insides were boiling, my legs were numb, and all I wanted to do was run. I didn't hide though.

I told them everything that happened this year (except for my panic attacks). From the disbelief of knowing someone personally who didn't listen to someone else's "No," to the divide that came within our community. After Loren's attempt, I told them how tired I was.

Before coming home for spring break, it had been hard to get out of bed. I stopped going to classes. I was behind on deadlines. The only thing I would do is go to work. Sara would turn on the lights in my room for me to get up.

Anyone could see the shock on *mami's* face. Open mouth, wide eyes, and disbelief.

Papi wanted to know more. What happened that his daughter almost left school?

After telling them, *mami* asked "Why didn't you tell us? We would have told you to come home. You can always come home."

Tears fell.

To share a truth I didn't want to admit was like letting a breath go that even I didn't know I was holding. This year has been hard, and I wasn't sure if I was going to make it to the end. I wanted to come home.

"I know if I had told you, I would have come home. I needed to finish it though. Staying in bed, not going to classes, not doing my work? That's not me. It's never been me. I needed to see it through. I came home and it gave me the strength to go back."

Mami tried to object - why put myself through that if I could come home?

"I knew I could come home. But I wasn't the only one going through it. I couldn't leave my friends. Patricia, Teresa, Sara... I wasn't going through it alone. We had all been trying to take care of each other. Built closer bonds because of everything happening on campus. I was raised to finish everything I start. I intend to do just that with college. But if I came home, it would be like giving up."

I almost gave up.

Saying it out loud though. Letting *mami* and *papi* know that I struggled helped. I felt like I could breathe easier. Maybe they'd understand why I slept so much when I first got back in May.

Sweets*
September 20, 2012 at 12:27 AM

Seated on the soft couch, I ate my blue cupcake. Looking around, I kept to myself like any good wallflower would. Surrounded by a group of people, yet still alone. Just enough noise, just enough presence to make others believe I was still around.

Big Boss: *You didn't fool everyone, Amira...*

I looked at the entrance and saw them. The two powerhouses that never failed to show me what love looks like. Patricia and Teresa looked my way, grabbed my plate of sweets and in silence, walked out.

I knew what it meant.

Sigh.

I get up and walk behind them.
Cheerleader: *Yes. Here we go.*

"What is going on Amira?" Patricia yells.

-   silence   -

"It's been seven days"

-   silence   -

"TALK to us. We gave you your days but talk to us. Let us help," Patricia pleads.

Slumped, with a trembling chin, I finally let the rain roll down my face. A crack of my voice comes out uttering the words, "I just don't know if I'll get past this." Speaking through the trembles and sobs, I shared with them that I made a decision that summer to not be a mother. I thought I could make the decision and be okay, but they saw something I refused to accept. Silent, talking to no one, I was not okay.

On the carpet, Teresa held me, cried with me, and told me "you made the decision best for you and it's okay. It's okay to be okay with the decision and still be upset about it." That was the issue I was struggling with though. Before making the decision, I hadn't thought that I would ever be okay with the decision, but I had been. That's what I was fighting. In her arms though, I felt like I could breathe again.

I said, "I never thought I would make that decision. And I'm sorry I haven't spoken to you two, but I just didn't know how to say it."

Holding me tighter, Teresa spoke to me and let me know she understood. It's like she knew what to say to comfort me, to let me know I wasn't alone. Sometimes, even when we do what's best for us, we get sad. That's exactly what I was, in that moment, sad. Finally, I got to say I was.

Patricia and Teresa held me, reminding me they were here for me. This is what friendship looked like; what sisterhood should feel like.

Deep breath in. I nod. I'm not alone and I didn't want others to feel alone either.

Love Note #17

Everyone has their own personal values and beliefs. When able to, we all make the decision we deem best for us.

If at any moment in your life, you have ever felt conflicted about a decision you made, know you made the best decision for you... There are moments in life and in history where sometimes people had choices taken away from them. That was not their fault. If a decision was taken from you, it was not your fault. At times when this happens, when it comes to making a choice for ourselves, it feels wrong, like we shouldn't be making a decision. Unapologetically and with no explanation or justification, if it's in your ability to do so, you have every right to make the decision you best deem for you.

Unconquered

September 25, 2012 at 1:58 AM

William Ernest Henley's words have stayed with me. Written so many years ago, and still recited today...

"Out of the night that covers me Black as the pit from pole to pole I thank whatever gods may be for my unconquerable soul"

Sigh.

I repeated this over and over again before going to therapy.

Walking through the two glass doors was difficult enough. Walking in meant taking a risk to having the unknown turn out horribly. I haven't considered the positive. For me, it's about: Could I really talk about everything going on in my head? Could I talk about what happened to me even though I didn't report? What if they judged me? What if they thought I was a risk to myself and sent me to the ER?

Now imagine walking in, only to find out they had errors in the system, and actually, I was never entered into the system. It meant I wouldn't have therapy today. Therapy's on campus but walking over was like walking through cement. There were days, like today, that felt impossible. All I could do was repeat the poem.

"Head up Amira. Walk out of here. It's a waste of time anyway," Big Boss would say sternly.
Look Out Lu chimed in, *"We don't need them."*
"No Amira, stay. Reschedule," said Cheerleader.

Shaking my head, I just wanted my mind to stop for a second. I needed a distraction from the fight, from Big Boss, Look Out Lu, and Cheerleader. I just wanted to be Amira. Amira - the one who didn't need therapy. Amira - the one who could be in crowds. Amira - the one who trusted people and let them love her.

Sigh.

I repeat the poem. Not wanting to focus on the urge to run, I repeat the poem. This poem, the one that I have said with people who have struggled with wanting to stay alive. This poem. I want to live. I'm trying to manage the panic and nervousness, my triggers. It doesn't help that my appointment was never scheduled.

Closing my eyes, I reminded myself to stay still instead of running out.

Cheerleader: *I am okay right now. YOU are okay right now. Breathe Amira.*

Look Out Lu: *Why is it so hard to make it here? Why do I have to say this poem? When will I not feel like I have to walk through cement to get myself here?*

I'm getting help though. There was an Irish, kind, gentle therapist inside who was not opposed to meeting with me. It wasn't his fault the system had glitches. I used the affirmation he helped me formulate in a previous session.

"You are more than what happened to you, Amira." - three times.

Breathe.

I'm not sharing everything, but I feel like I could. When I complete my therapy homework, I read what I chose to share in session. When I spoke, it was like driving 60mph on a 25mph lane. He would stop me like that of a stop sign that I tried to ignore. Having me pause, he taught me to not be afraid of my discomfort and tears. He stood. He guided me through grounding exercises. He reminded me, I got to share what happened because it happened.

In those moments, I was grateful for the Amira Luisa's in my head - Big Boss, Look Out Lu and Cheerleader.

The parts of me that looked to protect me would all say *Breathe Amira. Remember Invictus.*

We called the kind therapist Nathan.
"Let's go back to what you just said there"
Eyes in terror, I asked "what?"
"Go back a couple sentences. I couldn't understand because you were talking really quickly"
I gave him the look of "well you know why I'm saying it quickly" to which he replied "take your time. You are no longer there."

I talked about Sly Guy. Nathan knew there were certain things I had never thought of uttering out loud. At that moment, the therapist who told me I could change my mind came to me as if they were also in the room with me. Mr. Heart was there too - how he taught me: "just one part of my story." Here I was talking about the other part I had never said out loud.

Deep breath in... "It went on for months..."

85

It's taken me some time to accept the fact that I did what I could. In session, I said all that I could bring myself to say. I'm trying to not judge myself too much when I don't get through all of it. It is not easy.

It's frustrating to find out that on some days my session wasn't scheduled because I'm trying to find worth in living. But to be told "You can't be seen today" is like saying, I don't matter. Nathan reminds me I had a poem to recite. One I already know by heart.

In the moments like today where I'm told I have no appointment, I remind myself "my head is bloody but unbowed." I'm growing my ability to cope when things don't go according to plan. As I move forward, my coping mechanisms have changed; both behaviourally and emotionally. In turn, my triggers have changed too which is why unexpected or last-minute changes are sometimes difficult to handle. I'm beginning to see how my triggers differ at this age from when they were first formed.

Love Note #18

Give yourself credit. Even in moments, you think you aren't enough. Take this moment to reflect and think of all the things you have done today. Maybe not everything happened the way you wanted it to. Maybe it did. Maybe not all of it happened according to plan. Maybe it did. Maybe you didn't get to everything. Maybe you did. Either way, it's okay.

Timelines and deadlines will always exist. Work will always exist. People wanting things from you will continue to exist. At this moment, thank yourself for doing what you have done today. Give yourself credit.

Next

Another canceled session, another night, another guy.

It's happened three times over the last two months. That means almost half my sessions have been canceled without me asking for it to be or were never entered. I'm over it.

"You coming home with me tonight?"

Raised eyebrows, #5 looked at me. "Who are you?... What have you done to the Amira I know?"

"Like you weren't thinking about it. You just didn't expect ME to say it." I said laughing with the flirty eyes.

Grabbing my hand, he led me to the dance floor. #5 said, "Meet me at the door in an hour."

I knew what we were. From the first kiss to the last time we slept together, we were just one more body added to our lists. All I needed was something (or in this case someone) to help me forget the ick I felt in my body.

Next.

HoneyCurls, Next.
Salsero, Next.
Body Pillow, Next.

Never all at once but what a life where we (I) said, "We get our needs met and that's all. I require nothing else from you. Now you are dismissed. You can go now."

Close enough to achieve the physical touch I craved, far enough away to never be made to go through heartbreak or pain ever again.

There are feelings of loneliness, of shame, that I won't admit to. The extreme desire for no one to really look at me. If they do, they would see that I wanted exactly the opposite of what I am doing. I didn't know what would happen if someone actually asked me. The danger and fear I feel of having to answer.

Look out Lu: *Tell no one.*
Big Boss: *It's none of their business what you do.*
Cheerleader: *But it's okay to want a relationship.*
Look out Lu: *What! What are you saying? ... Do you know what could happen?"*
Cheerleader: *I'm just saying they don't have to just be one more body. God, we don't want people to think she's a slut either.*

Big Boss: *So, what if they do? She's entitled to say yes to whoever she wants.*
Cheerleader: *Yes, but why is she saying yes...You don't have to add bodies just to forget.*

Oh, how do I stop these conversations in my head?

Whatever. I'm not dealing with this.

Next.

Love Note #19

Even when we make a decision, the decision is still influenced by how we feel and think about something prior to the action. Similar to giving yourself credit in the last love note, take some time here. Have you ever struggled with something you yourself were doing? Maybe wanted to change, but didn't know how or weren't ready to change even if the desire existed? Maybe you continued to do that action even if you knew it was more so about avoiding something else?

Reflect on what's coming up for you. Is there something you've been avoiding? Do you avoid it because you feel hopeless, hopeful, empowered, victimized, intimidated or in control? Something else entirely? What would it look like if you didn't go to war with yourself? Is there anything you can say to the discomfort to ease it and let it know you are okay at the moment?

Hot Chocolate for the Heart
> January 20, 2013 at 12:52 AM

I looked at Eyebrows. "I don't want to do this anymore…"

"What are you talking about?"

"I don't even like doing it. Having sex, I mean. I feel nothing."

"So then why do it?"

Big Boss: *THAT's the big question isn't it.*

I, Amira Luisa, kept saying next. Onto another one. Yet I have had no connection to the guys, no desire to really be with them. With not one single drop of passion when I would say "Hey, I want you". *So why was I still having sex?*

Back to the books, I stared at the pages. Eyebrows got me thinking. Why was I doing this? Why add another body to my list?

Big Boss: *To say yes this time.*
Look out Lu: *You are the one saying yes.*
Cheerleader: *To forget someone didn't listen to your no.*
Big Boss: *To avoid thinking of the past.*
Cheerleader: *Forgive yourself... please.*
Look out Lu: *It is not her fault. She has to be like this...*

Has to?

Shaking my head, snapping back to reality, I realized Eyebrows was raising her hand at me.

"Amira, I don't know everything you have been through, but I can imagine there is a reason. But if you don't want to have sex, don't."

"I feel like I can't stop," I said with tears welling up. "Even when I don't want to, I still initiate it… I flirt and tell them I want them. When it is happening though, I feel like I'm not even there."

"Have you talked to anyone about this?"

With unstoppable tears, I shook my head. "No. I go to therapy but how can I admit what I'm doing? After everything I've been through to now willingly do it to myself... They'll think I'm crazy or an addict... Thank you Eyebrows for listening"

Eyebrows nodded and asked if she could give me a hug. All I felt was her gray fleece giving me a load of comfort – like if I had drank a hot chocolate after being out in the cold. It warmed my heart.

Love Note #20

It's not always the easiest thing to admit that we are hurting or that we've been hurt. Sometimes it is easier to stay with what we know. Do with what we know at that moment.

If at any point, a story is too much, take a step back. It's okay to put the book down. Call a friend, go for a run. Know that while at times things are heavy, new things have occurred as a result. For example, an awareness beginning to form after a conversation.

Now, it is possible to talk to someone, like a therapist, but not say EVERYTHING. It doesn't mean it has gone away, but a conversation is still happening somewhere. If you are having a conversation with yourself, maybe don't like the way it's going, see if there is a place or person you would like to have the conversation with. It's okay to want to lean on someone. It's okay if it remains with you too. It's a process.

Yet again

June 20, 2013 at 2:12 AM

Mr. Heart returned yet again. For the last five months, it's been good. He came back after… something ended. I thought he had gotten things figured out now. Believed that it was me he wanted.

We spent days together - sunny dates, sushi dates, pier dates. It was OUR summer.

Until it isn't. Again. That's what I'm back to thinking.
We are imperfectly perfect together. Walking on the sidewalk, I looked up and saw my first love staring back. I saw not only my first love, but a fear of attachment. Is he going to leave again? Will I?

Big Boss: *oof... if your girls knew...*
Cheerleader: *Leave her alone Big Boss!* Smiling she said, *she should fall in love again.*
Look Out Lu: *Are you crazy? Do you even remember what happened a few months ago?*

Ah yes... spring semester. What a trip. As if that wasn't a couple weeks ago...

I am not a safety net.

He said she was just a friend.

With limited availability, I saw a distance between us grow again. It was beyond the states that were already between us. The end was near and I felt it because my doubts had begun to grow again. The need to cry grew; the energy shifted. Our conversations were less frequent, shorter. I knew something was coming between us.

Having been a summer pastime two summers in a row, I had been clear. We were not tied to each other but yet my hopes have been lifted. I have let my guard down. But I'd be lying if I said I wasn't afraid of him leaving again.

So, I have gotten myself a Next... right after I found out indeed someone, not something, had come between us.

She was not new to the conversation. I got to see what possibilities looked like from someone else's eyes. Mr. Heart's eyes shined, his smile widened, slightly hesitant but hopeful.

Italiana was the reality check that we had been just a pastime then and probably now.

I saw him going for the home run but didn't say anything. He didn't either.

In March, my friends and I co-hosted a week of events and ironically, it was focused on love.
- What it looks like (platonic, familial, romantic)
- What's healthy and isn't
- What did we (I) want

Someone saw me. One of my girls who has been there but who I held at arm's length.

To the curly hair, tall-everyone-is-just-taller, fierce, hide-from-no-one leader, my best friend, I thank her for seeing me.

Our week of events had just ended, and I was curled up and crying. Patricia got my hands, brought me up from the floor and brought me up to the bed. It was the weekend of celebration for us and I had imagined it being joyous, fun, and exciting. One text had changed my entire mood and Patricia was not having it.

"This week you said you wanted a loving and happy love, where you could grow with someone and have fun... You took charge during the events in a way you haven't done before... Where is that Amira now?"

I stared at her. "When he returns, I feel like this. Like a doormat, like a safety net, someone he just turns to out of convenience because he knows I'll be there."

At that moment, it felt like everything had become clearer. Uttering those words out loud made me stop and hear myself. My first love showed me love didn't have to physically hurt but it was now trying to show me when a love was not serving me anymore.

We are strong. We will be okay without him.

"I don't want to feel like a safety net anymore. I don't want to be his safety net anymore"

I deserve more.

So, I walked away… well in this case stopped replying. So now, I have to decide.

Love Note #21

Ever have someone who just reminded you that you are one of a kind? No one has a right to hurt you or use you. You deserve to live free of harm.

If you have experienced that person, witnessed it offered to someone else, at this time: reach out and be that person to someone else. Or if you need that person, name someone it could be.

Italiana

November 30, 2013 at 2:34 AM

I thought the fight of first love being continued love was over. I had made a choice in June to give us a chance and five months later, it's back to being a rollercoaster. More dates, more worries. More doubts, more kisses. For some time, it felt like we might actually make it work…

until FB Messenger chimed one evening.

"Italiana has sent you a message"

Big Boss: *Breathe Amira.*
Inhale.
Look Out Lu: *But you can't hold it forever. Let it out.*
Exhale.
Cheerleader: *Don't open it. There's nothing you two need to talk about.*

94

Italiana: "Hey, Mr. Heart told me about what you two went through. I'm wondering, what were your symptoms?"

Confused, but soon realizing what she was talking about, it would seem we were at an impasse. Unsure what to do but just have the message be left on seen. It would appear that she, like I did, had to make a decision about being a mother. However, this was a decision I did not want to know existed.

Of all days, she would message me on my favorite holiday. Thanksgiving came and went like any other day. I told Cristal and Cat. They distracted me with Uno... Yahtzee... Monopoly...

I don't remember how the night after the games went or if I slept. I do remember getting the confirmation there was a decision to be made.

Tears. Tears. Some more tears.

Nope. Don't do that. Shut that off. You don't need him.

I know Big Boss. But I was sad.

Chicago, rom coms, and Starbucks
December 1, 2013 at 3:33 AM

I returned back to campus the day after all the tears. Dropped my bags and I felt my chest grow tight. Tears welling up with no gate or lockdown to stop them.

"Siri, call Sonny" Ring... no answer
"Siri, call Teresa" Ring... no answer
"Siri, call Patricia" Ring.. "hello"
I don't know whether it was words or sobs that came out of my mouth. I only knew that the empty house was not what I needed at the moment.

Patricia: "Breathe."

Grounding me, Patricia reminded me I was alive.

"You are still loved"

She said I wouldn't be alone for too long. I nodded, hung up confused. *But she is still in another state. What did she mean?*

Poeta showed up and was sitting with me five minutes later as I cried silently.

"I need to work on my thesis. It's the whole reason I came back early."
"Amira... it's okay. Not tonight. Right now, you can cry."

Big Boss found it necessary to whistle in my ear. *HELL NO. It's time to get down to business.*
Calm down. Give her this moment.
Lu, she has things to do. She shouldn't waste her time crying for him. It's over.
It stung but it was true.
Cheerleader stepped in. *As much as you may not want to feel this, you are. Feel this. Amira, cry. It's okay to cry.*

Sad and hurt, I was reminded I was not alone.

Distance had not stopped Patricia from answering just like it didn't stop her from calling Poeta. Poeta brought Curls and Lisa with her later that night. They held me as I cried but I was crying because of the romantic comedies we watched. Curls had given me the Grande Caramel Brulee Latte. It was just what I needed.

They stayed with me, held me, hugged me.

I wasn't alone.

I am loved.

La Rabia...

...is that boiling lava-like sensation inside of you, that's about to erupt.

There are still times where my anger seems too much to contain. It's constantly having to make the split-second decision of being *la mala educada (the bad-mannered)* or remaining the well-educated Latina I was raised to be.

Throw your phone. Flip tables.
No. Actually, cry. Scream!
Better yet, yell. Shout!
Punch! Punch something so hard that it, whatever IT is, breaks, says Big Boss.

No, we can't do that.
It's not socially acceptable, so...

Blink back the anger.
Swallow the rage.
Clench and unclench the bite.
Turn off your voice.

Now all it takes is a train delay. Someone pushing past me. But this is New York! It happens all the time. And it's not them, that I'm angry at...is it?

No.

Big Boss comes out now, but stronger than in the past.
Keep moving. Don't spend time in train stations.
The deep-rooted voice like from the movie, Inside Out, is speaking.
Listen to me.

Except it is not an emotion. Big Boss, I now realize, is my mask; the mask that protects me from feeling too much pain at a train station.

The one that is afraid that if we rest, it'll be too much. Our world, our story will be too much. So much that it can't be held in.

Big Boss is also the one who says: *Just stop already.*
How long has it been? Five? Na. Eight years?
Almost TEN YEARS! GET OVER IT.
Why aren't you over this already?!

Here comes Cheerleader though… *BREATHE.*

Glaring at Big Boss, Cheerleader loves generously and validates ferociously. *It's okay, love. You can make it until the next train comes.*

Big Boss: *C'monnnnn… we've got things to do!*
I looked at my watch on my left wrist, and heard:
Break or throw the phone already, so we can move past this.

And suddenly, Look Out Lu arrived.
Nah, don't spaz out. They'll lock you up if they knew…if they saw!

"What would happen if I break down in one of these situations of mine?"

Look Out Lu: *They'll think you're crazy! That's what.*
Listen to me. You can't have them looking at you like --
Big Boss: *Can't let that happen. You're better now.*
Got things going for you. So, go do them!… please

Cheerleader: *Hush now… breathe Amira.*
Be kind to yourself. This happens. Time is a construct.
Many years can pass, and it can still impact you.
Remember to give yourself credit for how far you've come.

Sometimes I feel like I don't make sense. How do I tell myself one thing - only for another part of me to say something different? Who do I listen to? Who do I listen to when all those voices are me?

There are moments that I believe I'm still at the train stations all those years ago. I'm crying on the train ride home. It's as if I'm still living in the past. The panic of not knowing what will happen, will we get caught; my mind is constantly fighting the panic.

La Rabia: The frustration I feel within myself of not saying no, enough.

The self-blame. I know I'm no longer there but it's like my mind is playing tricks with my heart... It's like a heartbeat. Sometimes it's in a consistent rhythm; sometimes it's an irregular heartbeat. Sometimes it is beating too quickly that one may think the person is having trouble breathing. Or having a heart attack.

However, things are different now. I'm working in my field of choice; doing the work I want to do & meeting new people. I'm in a beautiful relationship and yet...here I am... still feeling an inexplicable sense of anxiety and irritability.

Inhale.

Don't worry Amira, you can do this.
So, defuse the bomb in the back of your throat.
Let the tears water the garden of your eyes.
Release the tension of your hands.
Breathe...as if you were smelling the sunflowers,
Or blowing out the candles of your birthday cake...
Congratulations my dear!
You have lived through this one more day, says Cheerleader.

Exhale.

"What would happen if I lost control? If I let loose?"
"What if letting loose meant I would be living?"

I don't know. The fear of the unknown was too much. That's why Cheerleader comes out.

You can do this Amira. Keep going. Scared or not, she says.

"I can't."

Oh, but you can, mama. Believe in yourself.
Closing my eyes, I board the train.

V: The Courage to Live

I, Amira Luisa, am loved.

I choose love.

And.

I choose differently **now**.

My story continued with a couple more sad experiences but each with lessons learned.

From the age of twelve, I moved with the mentality "all I say I am going to do, all I start, I will achieve. I will finish. Always. I don't start anything I can't finish."

At the same time, I denied myself the opportunity to dream. It's like having terrible eyesight vision and someone giving me someone else's prescription. I could only go as far as I could see all the while missing the lane that was really meant for me.

The battle of "why dream, because what I want won't happen" began.

A little over ten years later though, after some of my most painful memories, I got myself the right prescription.

I chose differently.

It started with love and integrity.

Love,   January 17, 2019

To see youth in the classroom,

Forming bonds.
Creating projects.
Teaching to expand the minds and hearts.
Providing as well as receiving information.

I, Amira Luisa, was where I needed to be.

With the youth.

Then came integrity.

The choice to stay or walk away from what did not serve me
again arrived.

Integrity,   March 22, 2019

"Amira doesn't do anything"
I do things but you just want me to do it your way.

"Why am I paying her if she does nothing?"
You don't write my paychecks though.

"She is not thorough with her work"
*Alright lady, you want to talk about my work. You don't do my job.
Don't come in here telling me how to do my job that you don't know
how to do.*

"It's time for you to go"

   -   silence   -

No.

"I give the last say. Leave"
There will be a day you can't kick me out from where I belong.

I leave.

Sunshine and glasses,   April 13, 2019

It was time to go so I went.

Still working with youth, yet unsatisfied. Something was missing.

Work became dreaded. Difficult to get out of bed. Tears every day.

If there's one thing I definitely do not do is – I, Amira Luisa, do not
'not love' what I do.

A conversation with Patricia ensued from leaving
and being unsatisfied.

"Trust me and take a chance on yourself"

I did. I chose differently and I had no idea what I was stepping into.

Sunshine came into my life telling me who I was, telling me about
myself, refusing to let me slide. Who was this man and who did he
think he was?

Sunshine: "Take off your glasses"

Excuse me. What? – Panicked Look Out Lu says.
Gulp. – Big Boss

"Let us see you without your glasses. Show yourself."
 "Na, I can't see past my hands without them."

"That's okay. We'll see you through. You are used to using your glasses to hide."

Stop.
Wow.

Alright now Amira. Shake it off like a duck.

Big Boss: *Lets GOOOOO*
Look Out Lu: *C'mon now! You know you don't back away from a challenge*
Cheerleader: *Hush now… Let her hear this. This. This is necessary.* Smiling. *Go Amira, be seen.*

Taking off my glasses, I started to cry tears… of relief? It felt like it was the opening night of a show and the curtains were being open for the very first time. I spoke for the first time with true honesty and vulnerability as Sunshine asked what it was that I wanted.

"What I have realized in these last few days is I want to travel. To have a family. To build a life with someone. To create memories with them filled with happiness, love and a whole lot of trust."

YASSSSS goes Cheerleader.
Breathing and clapping goes Look Out Lu.
Smiling and nodding goes Big Boss.

Finally.

From living life passively, listening to all the doubts and fears, I, Amira Luisa, at that moment chose differently.

At that moment, I began to choose love – to have it, to be it, to give it (not only to others but also myself).

I chose to do it even though I was scared.

I chose to dream and to say it out loud.

It started with getting the right prescription of glasses.

Live,   April 16, 2019

What does it mean to live?

Is it to ignore everything that's happened? *No.*

Is it to pretend it never happened? *Right, because when has that ever worked.*

Is it to hold IT (the memories, the emotions, the experiences) by its hand and say "I got you. I will dream and create better moments for you"? *Maybe.*

I choose this.

To create a life worth living – surrounded by family, a love that is fun, committed, loving, and joyful, with a passion that is ignited and reinforced every day, like that one day when I was 21.

The day I met Amita.

Amita,   April 19, 2019

Amita, the two-year-old, dark brown curls, little fighter.

Thank you.

At 21, Amita reminded me what every little girl deserves to have.

- Joy
- A voice
- Fierce love for self that looks like "that attitude" that says "you can't tell me nothing"

Her mom taught her to go get what she wanted. If someone told her, "you can't have [this], you go get it and say, "I deserve [this]"

If she wanted something, like a set of markers, and no one wanted to give it to her, she crawled to it. Crawled and climbed onto the chair, onto the desk, and crawled her way to the middle of the table to get it.

What. A. Powerhouse.

I saw her heading down the hall without her mom. I let her mom know.

"Don't worry, let her go. If she goes too far, she'll return. She'll let me know if she needs me."

It was another example of her believing in Amita while still letting her grow in her own beauty, individuality, and strength.

It was similar to when she told me, "I have a name card for her." I stood in admiration.

Name card?

A name card – so people will always know who she was and where her name came from. No one could get close to her if they did not know how to pronounce her name.

I said to myself, *I want to be able to raise a little girl like that one day.*

Me. The one who at that time said wouldn't and didn't want to have kids. Me.

Back then, I wasn't ready.
(I'm still not. But I can dream now)

I choose differently now.

I choose to remember my dream that scared me; that I refused to accept.

I choose to remind myself that I, too, can have a daughter, believe in her, do my best to keep her safe while letting her live her life. I can build a bond with her where she knows her mom will always show up for her and life will happen, but she is not alone.

Love Note #22

The journey continues. It isn't over but you've gotten to see what she has gone through. Thank you. Know your journey, whatever journey you are on, continues too. Every day. It can have inner battles, love, joy, disappointment, and so much more. It continues. Trust that.

A letter to my insecurities,   April 22, 2019

Thank you.

For keeping me safe during the times I felt I had to BEWARE.

This is not that anymore.

To the alarm system that tells me to stay away from every kind of love, I get it. I get you. I get why you came to be. You didn't want to see me be hurt again.

But Big Boss...my alarm system...I want to love. I am enough.
I know I still question it sometimes.

I am learning to love myself again.
Every day, in all ways, always.

It's not easy but I'm doing it.

Alarm system, what can it be like to allow someone else to love me too?

To the fear that says and asks if I will ever be enough:
I ask you: to who? For who?

Look Out Lu.

For me, I know I am still here even after days I thought I couldn't bear it anymore. From the days I thought of ending it all. From the days where I waited to die. I have found ways and continue to find ways to keep going. To live, just a bit more. To explore and remain curious.

I am enough. For me. The life I am creating is mine. I get to say and choose to include others. To be seen even when scared.

That is what I'm choosing now.

To cautious love and good vibes, thank you for supporting me, for encouraging me to be there for others and for supporting me in finding a reason to live.

Cheerleader.

I know you had doubts. I get why you stayed quiet during the moments you saw the decisions I was making hurt me. You let me see on my own that wasn't love nor good vibes. I'm ready now though. To love without being overly cautious.

I honor the fact that you all exist.
You came to me in the times I needed you most.
Parts of me will continue to need you.

I won't push you away. Come with me though.
Stay with me and let me know when danger, real danger, is near.
Be my lookout. Cheer me on when you know I am creating the life I

truly want. Remind me and tell me who is the boss of her own life.

However, all I ask is that YOU listen to me TOO.

I know the doubts, the fear, the questions, the panic will come and go, change and reappear in different forms when I least expect it. I ask you, insecurities, trust me. Trust I can handle it.

I trust the detours will lead me where I am meant to go.

I choose to go.
I choose to live.
I choose to create.
I choose to dream.
I choose to act.
I choose to be.
I choose to say yes to myself.

12-year-old Amira,   May 9, 2019

I'm proud of you for surviving.

I. am. proud. of. you.

You had something happen to you that should have never occurred. You weren't wrong to stop trusting. You did what you needed to do.

You kept yourself safe. Protecting the once chubby cheeks, always smiling, goofy-angelic face little girl. Making sure no one touched her. You hid her away, understanding that little girl was worth more. Deserved better and would always be more than what was done to her.

You followed directions so you wouldn't draw attention.

Attention meant danger. No attention meant staying safe. Silence filled your throat out of love, not just shame. 12-year-old Amira, you know now that was not your shame to carry. It was not your fault.

You loved people who were supposed to keep you safe or at least care for and look out for you. Silence came to be in order to prevent more pain. What happened after was also not your fault.

I'm proud of you. You learned to watch out for danger, to fight for what you wanted. This led you to 21-year-old Amira.

21-year-old Amira, May 23, 2019

Forgive yourself. Most importantly, love yourself.
You didn't know it would happen again.
You did what you could with what you knew at 15.
What you know at 21 will also change again.

To 15-year-old Amira first: Forgive yourself.

Forgive yourself for having said okay in the beginning. For not asking for clarification. You didn't know what sex was at the time so how could you ask about something you didn't think of. Forgive yourself for not screaming, for not yelling, for not telling someone. Forgive yourself for it taking months to finally say enough. You said enough. When it was time, you said enough.

Forgive yourself for being prepared to die. At that time, you didn't think any other way could bring about different results. Let alone safety or healthy love.

Be kind to yourself for not saying something. It's still hard on some days to accept that it occurred for months. You said no. You walked away. You cried. You were sad but you continued.

21-year-old Amira: You thought you didn't deserve happiness, to exist, to be loved, to belong. This is what happens when something that should have NEVER happened, happens. Feeling lost, alone, hopeless, and disconnected from yourself and the world happens. The 'being hard on yourself' happens. The people who didn't know or refused to see the beauty in you worked overtime to make you believe you were nothing. Sweet darling, you are everything.

Be kind to yourself, because even then, even though it was and still is at times hard to see, you are so much more. Forgive yourself for the mistakes you made in relationships. Making mistakes is a human thing to do. No one is perfect.

Forgive yourself for avoiding open, loving, vulnerable, intimate relationships. When things that should have NEVER happened occur, it makes it difficult to have, to build, and to believe in relationships.

Be kind to yourself for the decisions you make after the fact. Saying "next" and "we only get our needs met" -- that happens. You did what you could with what you knew then.

You are not crazy. You. are. Not. a. Terrible. Person. You are not a terrible person for having sex and feeling nothing.

Forgive yourself for the argument you had with yourself. For the moments you were mean to yourself, saying hurtful things to yourself. You did take many risks in "engaging in promiscuity" but you did what you needed to do. Even if it didn't feel good. Even if it did.

Forgive yourself for not trusting. For believing you had to be an army of one. You knew -- you had people by you -- even if you held them at arms... legs length.

You fought for yourself, for your own chances even when people had their doubts.

Forgive yourself for your inner battles. For the nights that those inner battles became physical and you ate anything in sight. Forgive yourself for hating yourself afterward every time you did it.

Be kind to your anger. It's kept you moving. The days it came out were the days you were telling yourself "you still can. You still have it in you to keep going."

You may have gotten annoyed with mom or dad, a boss, or a friend. But you also listened.

Just like you kept people at arms... legs length, you still took chances throughout the years. You formed some bonds that didn't last (but others that DID).

When they yelled at you because you wouldn't share, you listened. Then, you shared when you were ready. When you knew they would hold you.

Forgive yourself for feeling sad even on the good days. 12-year-old Amira was watching over you just. in. case.

Forgive yourself for speaking low -- in classrooms, at work, among peers. We never know how people will respond to us. We only get to choose what parts of us we want to show them.

Forgive yourself for making yourself invisible and small.

You are neither. Be seen.

Love letter to Amira, June 6, 2019

Amira, stay brave. You have made it this far and you will continue to go farther. Life has not been easy. It has been kind as well as cruel. Amira, continue to stay brave. Listen to your heart. Do what you want to do. Be brave and take the step you want. Take the step even if you are not sure how it will turn out. Trust your dream, your vision, yourself. You deserve for your dreams to come true.

Amira, stay curious. Look for what interests you. Never settle. Try new things even if you are terrified. Jump. Like the day you went on the Cyclone. Wooden and old roller coaster. Afraid of heights and all, you went. Jump.

Stay inspired. You are surrounded by creatives… By amazing people and works of art. Life will life. Look towards what and who uplifts you. Have them serve as a reminder that YOU ARE ALIVE. To the ones who never let you go. Who have shown you that YOU ARE AMAZING. Who have shown you that YOU ARE NOT ALONE. Also, to the people, places, and things that have shown you love does exist. Peace and safety can exist. Risk does not always mean danger. It can also mean excitement.

Amira, do it scared. It won't always be easy. You won't be fearless but do it anyways. Choose you. Trust you. You have so much to offer this world. Let them see you. Most importantly, see yourself. You are not small. You are a powerhouse. YOU ARE ALIVE and LIVING.

Amira, show your treasures. What you have is beautiful. Don't hide. You have seen what you can do in your life already. Look at all you have accomplished. It is for you, by you. Now you get to share it.

Amira, don't quit. Keep going. You have many things you want to do. Even when you said you stopped dreaming, it was there. Your dreams just hid for a while until you were ready to bring them out. You are ready. Don't forget that.

Amira, LIVE. Keep living. Waiting to die is a thing of the past. Days will be hard. I'm not saying it all goes away. There will be times you may still cry, still want to deny. Take it by the hand and say, "I hear you" and "I'll take care of you until you know we are better now." Not every day will be great, but you get to live great moments. Keep going, keep living.

Amira, say YES to yourself. Others will want to keep you out. They may want to possibly use what you have been through against you. Pshhhh… that has already been done and you lived. You are still here. Say yes to you and fight for you as you have always done. The difference now is that it is not from a place of fear. Amira, you deserve to be seen. You deserve to have the life you want. There is nothing wrong with going for it. If others want to keep you out, fight. Fighting doesn't have to mean joining them. It can mean creating your own space or going somewhere else. You are worth so much more than someone else's no.

Amira, be unapologetic and do without permission. Go get what is yours. If it doesn't exist, create it. Love what you do. Take care of what you have. Stay grateful. But never forget, you get to go get yours! There will always be people who tell you no or want to take away your 'yes.' Fight and do it anyways. You don't need to wait for someone to tell you yes. Just like when you said you'd get enough money to go away for college. You did it. Go do it.

Amira, keep creating whatever your heart desires. Family, love, connection, wealth, joy, art, writing. Anything. Just keep creating.

Amira, dream BIG. If you can, do it easily, dream bigger. Go out of your comfort zone. Take that chance on yourself. Like the day you took off those glasses and went to go get the right ones.

Amira, stay open to possibilities. Stay open to the possibility of having things work out. You don't need to plan everything or control everything. Allow others to support you and lean on them. Those who can, will hold you. You deserve to be held. Don't let fear keep you from taking a chance. You know what I mean about fear. The fear that it'll happen again. The fear that you won't be listened to. You did what you could with what you knew then. You know differently now. Choose differently. But remember, you choose.

Amira, rejection, criticism, being misunderstood, overlooked, will occur. That's okay. DO it anyway.

Remember how others react to you is not yours to manage. Do you!

Don't forget the fear. Take it for the ride and YOU drive. Stay in the driver's seat.

Amira, fail. For all the love in you, fail. Fail so you can find another way that works for you. Failing doesn't mean failure. It means growth. You may not win the game, but you will gain experience.

Amira, you deserve community.
You deserve love.
You deserve freedom.
You deserve joy.
You deserve passion (I mean... HELLO)

Amira, continue to stand for yourself and give yourself the YES.

Dream. Dream BIG and wide. Take up space so that when fear, doubt, and worries come in, dreams will hold them while dreams still continue to push you forward.

Choose differently than what you used to know.

Choose NOW.

Most importantly, choose YOU.

Always.

Love Note X

Take a moment to honor any survivor you know. Hold them in your heart and accept that they may be on their own journey. Offer love, grace, and understanding.

Epilogue

Thank you for taking this journey with me. The idea for this book came to me around 2015. Amira's story, her personality, her individuality, her pain, her laughs, and her cries are all too real, too common.

From living an innocent life where all she knew was family and school drama, to learning what it meant to be frozen in fear and at an early age know what the desire to not fail others anymore was like. Amira took on a pressure placed upon her that she was to blame for all the bad things that happened to her. She entered high school where she again faced trauma that had her question what love really was. Coming to believe love was pain but fighting with a duality that love was also caring. She had people in her life that showed they only wanted what was best for her but fighting it because she didn't understand that there were people who wanted to harm her and that wasn't love.

It took years for Amira to understand both can exist at the same time. La Rabia or anger came to exist with time. All too often, people talk about how things just happen. their reactions just happen but Amira's story and the transition is meant to show that it's a build-up. Feeling both love and hate...joy and pain... And not understanding that both can exist simultaneously. So, La Rabia comes in. The battle of giving in to the anger but remembering that little sense of peace that will help settle it down in the moment. Self-awareness begins to grow as to why she does things the way that she does. She begins to question and ask questions. To demand and to say the things she wants. Some things she believes she deserves, and some are silenced. Some demanded self-protection and others started to create a mask of strength. Amira is resilient.

She has survived but it wasn't until she was ready to step forward courageously and live her life that she embraced this aspect of herself. Thank you for taking the journey with her. Reading about her life, her experiences, her lessons.

This book is for people who want a glimpse into the journey of healing from sexual violence. Too often we get stuck on the story of what happened to a survivor. This is the story of what happened, but it's also meant to be more, what came out of it for Amira. What she wants the world to know. It's never a survivor's fault.

I wrote this book for survivors to know healing can look many different ways, no way is THE way. It's for families and friends of survivors to delve into what battling… healing can look like and how trauma changes how relationships are formed but love above all, empathizing above all.

BELIEVING above all else supports survivors. The book was created with a lot of love in mind in the hopes of highlighting a little more just how much the journey of healing and moving forward consists of.

I write for the individuals who have gone through something they had no say in. For the folks who may not have put it into words for anyone but themselves. I write for our youth, telling them to show up freely as themselves, unapologetically. For the women and children who have trusted me with their story, their heart, and their mind.

I am a powerful, passionate, open, and loving leader and I'm committed to creating a world where individuals can live their life freely, where they are heard, and loved fiercely. A world where violence isn't internalized but challenged in order for our future generations to live the way they want. Thank you for being a part of this journey.

This book is for everyone. In reading this book, I like to think you joined me in the ride of Life. To understand what one fight can look like. A fight to live, to love, to understand, to grow. We are more than our story. Our story does not encage us. If we let it, it can free us.

Every day, every year of our lives (I choose to believe) is a new chapter. A story is being told. Every inner battle is a journey within itself, just like our battle with our outside life. Those journeys that are unseen deserve to be recognized.

~ Natalie Yaipen

References

Henley, W. E. (1888) Invictus. England: Book of Verses.

Peck, M. S. (2002) The Road Less Traveled: A New Psychology of Love, Traditional Values, and Spiritual Growth. New York: Simon & Schuster.